a Second Life

Stephen wright

First published in Seizure by Xoum in 2017

Xoum Publishing
PO Box Q324, QVB Post Office,
NSW 1230, Australia

www.seizureonline.com
www.xoum.com.au

ISBN 978-1-925589-04-7 (print)
ISBN 978-1-925589-05-4 (digital)

Cataloguing-in-publication data is available from the National
Library of Australia

Internal design and typesetting © Xoum Publishing 2017

Cover illustration and design by Sam Paine, www.sampaine.com
Printed in Australia by Lightning Source

Edited by Genevieve Buzo

*Viva la Novella V was made possible through the generous support of Xoum
Publishing.*

a Second Life

Our dreams are a second life. I have never been able
to penetrate without a shudder those ivory or horned
gates which separate us from the invisible world. The
first moments of sleep are an image of death; a hazy
torpor grips our thoughts and it becomes impossible
for us to determine the exact instant when the 'I',
under another form, continues the task of existence.
— Gerard de Nerval
Aurelia

There must be a secret hidden in this book
or else you wouldn't bother to read it.
— Kathy Acker
On Delany the Magician

|

Acker looks into the night sky above the silhouettes of the Rocks. The constellation of the Two Mothers, ringed by their campfires, floats above her like an enormous skeletal kite sailing on a vast and unfelt wind. She sits in the dark for a long time, so long that the wallabies that are as common as mice, and generally as timid, go thumping past her squabbling.

Acker doesn't sleep anymore. She just falls into dreams unannounced, aware of her body in space, sitting under the stars, while the dreams consume her. The dreaming that Acker used to carry so boundaried has vanished. Now she is like a fissure in space through which the dead fuse briefly with their own discarded memories, a pool into which they sink their unbearable states of loss and sorrow.

She takes the thing that is not herself, that has no owner but without which she is barely a husk, and jams open the space-time binomial. That is to say, she takes the beast that is the 'I' and enters the crevice where violence disappears, where the murdered have been thrown.

Acker remembers her last sleeping dream. She is standing outside the door of the room where she used to write, the desk with too many drawers by the window from which she could look down on the street; its junkies, broken cars, the sex workers she chatted with on the way home. Dusk is falling. The door slowly opens. A large hole the size of a cannon ball has been punched through the wall beneath the window, and through the hole a wind is blowing. The room is empty. A few dead leaves scutter about. And even in the dream it seems perfectly obvious that her life has become a desolate room, violently and mysteriously emptied.

Since then, all her patient, dangerous, lonely work has been predicated on her discoveries about memory: Memory is dream not history. Memory is a kind of slipshod grammar of dreams improvised out of whatever is lying around. It is cobbled out of bits of wreckage, spare parts, of insides and outs, the doors and windows and walls of the world, an archipelago of interiors and landscapes, perhaps not quite a map, perhaps closer to the archipelagos we might imagine when we gaze at evening cloud, our minds distracted from the evils of the day.

As she sits under the Two Mothers, Acker dreams of the journey she is going to make; its uncertain progress, the waypoints that continually shift, the topographies that undergo catastrophic transformation. Of course, the dead are not gathered in one place like tourists. The lands of the dead are many, so very many, layered on top of one another like leaves on a forest floor and can be like burned cinders or bowls of ash or endless winding tunnels. And there are those lands that Acker cannot enter, sealed off to her like old trunks. But, regardless of the destination, the journey always begins the same way: a ship of prisoners or slaves, packed in cages that grind against each other. For a long time the voyage is marked with the smell of burning and a moving strip of sky that slowly fills with ash.

—

In the morning Acker sits in the cabin of her red Ford F100 truck on the ridge above the valley, a fracture in the rim of the great caldera that reaches to the sea. The rain has cleared toward the dead distant volcanic stub of Wollumbin, the Cloud-Bringer. The valley is filled with a lake of white mist from which rise the colossal menhirs of the Rocks, the burial grounds for the Clever Men of the Widjabul people, their secret caves still guarded by the little spirit called the Nmbngee, whose gaze sweeps the entire valley.

The Rocks are the southern gateway to the little village, now drowned in the lake of mist, that sits on the rim of the green caldera like a broken cup fallen among a scree of mossy stones and whose northern gateway is the massive hump of the mountain known as Blue Knob. At the top of Blue Knob, hidden in the mist and the deep forests, is a cliff. A Widjabul woman of great power once lived up there alone. The Widjabul Clever Men visited her and to prove they had learned what she had taught them, the men had to jump off the cliff one by one and allow themselves to slowly drift to the ground. Some fell like stones. Of course, we are told, the woman used her power to guide them to the ground so that they wouldn't be hurt.

Asking what happens when we die is to ask both what death is, and what it is that dies. For Acker, it is cut and dried: people hang around.

But just as in a dream when one is confronted with a radioactive desert populated with all-night supermarkets and accepts the new landscape without a thought of the waking life they have left behind, so the dead, Acker has discovered, are pitched into a state they instantly fit themselves to. Death has no geography. It is an empty force gathering up all the particles of identity and memory, blowing through them without pause as their true nature is nakedly revealed: fabricated and transient and falling apart. Death is that moment when everything is uncovered and you fall into it, like a stone off a cliff.

How you die matters. Almost as much as who you were. When Acker re-read Dante she was struck by the familiar sense of claustrophobia and the ineluctable chains of cause and effect. And though the topology of Hell makes no more sense than the idea of just and eternal punishment or afterlives as ordered and regulated as the departments of local government, she acknowledges that the force of memory can propel one into places one would prefer not to go, places over which one has no control but that absorb one as completely and gently as a dream, a state whose boundary it is impossible to pinpoint.

Acker seeks out and follows the trails of violence. Violence has an infinite capacity to make itself invisible so that even when its effects are catastrophic, the field from which it arises effaces itself so completely that the violent act seems to float in space, split off from reality, like a bubble that has created itself.

And the village like every rural village across the country, is the entrance to a history of violence, dense with time and creaking under the weight of what has been done in its name, because nothing is forgotten. Every fragment of debris is evidence of the violence of the past. And as investigation is always the tracking and discovery of the past, a past that no one wants remembered, least of all the person asking about it, investigation is the beginning of a series of exhumations. And giving people what they say they want — what they say they have lost — always involves walking them slowly through a disaster area.

Acker guns the motor of the truck and is soon swallowed up in the fog . . .

. . . that at the bottom of the valley hangs suspended in the village street. A submarine silence. The rising sun is a long dissolved tear of yellow light. Blue Knob's dark mass looms out of the mist as though the village is about to be run down by an enormous lightless ship. The grumbling of Acker's red F100 can be heard as if at the end of a long tunnel. From the cassette player Strummer sings 'Armagideon Time'.

The truck swings into the desolate carpark, currently occupied by a single car, an ancient grey Camry. Interstate number plates. Acker can see the wide circles on its bonnet where the engine heat has burned off the night's condensation. Two children's seats in the back. A mother's mess of clothes and tissue boxes and bills.

Acker's boots crunch on the gravel as she walks up the alleyway to her office. She jingles her keys. A friendly sign. A bell tolling.

Her office is behind the Emporium, the village supermarket. It is not much more than a cupboard tacked onto the back of the Emporium's store rooms, the door sprayed with old graffiti tags. And it is here, leather-jacketed, cowboy-booted, chained, tattooed, earringed and pierced, with hair shaved and bleached, and a t-shirt so faded that the slogans printed on it read like a palimpsest, that Acker sits and broods and smokes and wonders why in all the streets in all the towns and suburbs and villages of the earth she has found herself sitting in this one. I visited Australia *once*. And now I'm glued here. It's the light, she thinks later, and the history of murder and the addiction to brutality and exploitation. It's as though I was sucked in by some sort of tidal karma. You have to be someone who thinks of what has been done to Australia and wants to vomit to be able to write of Australia, to understand what kind of writers it needs.

Acker waits for the secret life of the world to manifest, for women to come to her with their choking griefs, their desperation and their fury, that run beneath the day's inevitable passing like water beneath ice.

Acker no longer has the imagination to elaborate on herself anymore. It seems to her that in thinking of the past she is only perpetuating herself for herself. Her own mind is like a membrane splitting her from her own past, its chaos and its nausea. She still has glimpses as brief as sparks of what happened to her, the space between then and now, of the worlds she travelled. They are like memories of memories, like tableaux behind glass, relentlessly lit and spastically and mechanically repeating: rain on tumbled heaps of dumbfounded brick and splintered timbers; a city and its cargo of dead, in every hole and crevice burned bodies stacked in corners, buried in underground rooms, scattered like litter, as numerous as stones.

She thinks of that strange Australian TV show for preschoolers she saw one morning in her hotel room in Sydney shortly before she was to find out she was about to be eaten alive by cancer. Death as the Round Window in *Play School*.

Christ almighty, she says, out loud. Aren't you just a ray of fucking sunshine.

In crime fiction it is often the villages and small towns that hide a sinister sub-structure of violence and transgression, ringing the cities like refugee camps and harbouring an endless pro-liferation of terrorists, serial killers, cults, sexual predators and people smugglers. Those who fic-tionally murder often have no motive except to rejoice in their demonic cleverness. But this is the common daily crime: a man kills a woman, or a man kills her children, or a man kills a woman and her children. Or a man kills a woman and her children and then kills himself.

The dark and bloody tales of crime fiction, Acker thinks, are just descriptions of the ways we prefer to hide the truth or leave cryptic stupid clues about violence; that it's not just men who are messed up — though of course they are — but that all of us have been drawn into a vast, intricately built, prosaic, systemic structure of bloody-handed violence and murder, with only

STEPHEN WRIGHT

one prayer: Everything is property and therefore everything is exploitable.

And tracing the origin of its politics through the catastrophes of imperialisms that rolled over continents like tsunamis, the fascisms that were their scorched-earth response to its collapse, one always finds the dead giveaway, its dark heart, the dense point of its existence, over which one stumbles, like someone wandering in the darkness tripping over obstructions that turn out to be a shallow graves: It hates and fears a mother, any mother or any person who could become a mother *if she chose*; the being who can grow another being within her, transgressing the numinous principle of exploitation. The terror of the Real is this: All women are born of women. Men are not born of men.

A young woman is sitting on the steps outside Acker's little office wearing a t-shirt, skirt and Doc Martens. Her arms are wrapped around her knees and her face is red with cold. There are dark crescents like bruises under her eyes.

Acker says, You must be freezing.

The woman stands up awkwardly, moving off the steps so Acker can open the door.

Been waiting long?

She hesitates. No, she says. Her voice is quiet, devoid of affect. She doesn't look at Acker.

Once inside, Acker kneels to the ancient kerosene heater. Blue flame. She adjusts the heater,
leans back in her chair, cocks a boot heel on one
knee. A mirror hangs behind and above her, and
another hangs above the door in which Acker,
sitting opposite, can see herself, watching herself,
watching the other.

Okay, says Acker.

People said you would help.

Acker waits. Waiting, she thinks, I'm always
waiting. But then again, it's not like I can put it
on a brochure, she thinks: I will find your dead
children.

Acker listens, and hears the bones of the too-
familiar story, all the repetitive tropes of misogy-
nist violence: that to be is to own, that punishment
is justice, and if punishment is justice, murder is
transcendent justice, the sacrifice of martyrs.

The stalking. The threats. The ongoing terror.
How the cops did nothing. And the courts said,
The Father. The final text message. Her panicked
rush through the suburbs with a yawning chasm
tearing open her heart. Flinging open the screen
door. Blind in the gloom after the summer street.
Then the children's bodies, broken, blood like a
plant's shadow. How she noticed everything and
can't forget. Every detail. The body of the little
girl resting on her last out breath. The tiny scar

above her right eyebrow, the result of an infant fall. The dirt in the fold of skin beneath her chin. The runnels and smears of grime over her face where she had cried, wiped her face, and cried again. Her seamed eyelids. The boy slumped on the couch, his face white and calm as a mask. There was a little speck of blood on his hand, she says. Just a speck.

Acker waits and waits until the woman raises her head and looks her in the eye. Acker says quietly, Come back in the morning.

It's a business-like transaction in some ways. The grieving don't have time for small talk. Acker doesn't ask for introductions, exchange gossip or summarise the service options.

When the young woman has gone, Acker waits for the rush of cold air she's let in to settle. She picks up the deck of cards on the table beside her chair, shuffles them thoughtfully, lays them down, cuts and spreads them. Nothing has changed:

Bear what you can that others can't;

Try not to go crazy with it all;

Do it alone;

You are so fucked;

And no one cares.

After a few moments Acker locks the door behind her and goes out to find a cup of coffee.

Sometimes when Acker leaves her office it is

as if she is going out into an unfamiliar world. At dawn the light may be cold, the sky full of rain, the buildings clumped together like weeds. A car stuttering by. But an hour later, if she goes out again, everything is flat and pristine as if freshly painted onto a backdrop of blue, the street crowded with intent and fantastic figures, the hum of machinery rising into the sky. It is as if she has entered the street of a royal city.

And then sometimes she pushes open the door into an empty wasteland across which the wind blows unceasingly and the setting sun throws an eerie light into her eyes.

And at night . . .

Sometimes in the morning, Acker cannot remember the nights at all. She comes out of a dream and is lying on the floor, her clothes giving off the smell of burning.

The peeling facades of the village street, like sketches by Dr Seuss, are barely visible through the fog. Acker bangs on the closed door of the café.

—

In the office, Acker's cigarette stub is still smouldering a little in its ashtray. We see that three walls are lined floor to ceiling with precarious brick-and-plank shelves crammed with books. The timber floor is swept clean. The straw broom stands in the angle between two shelves. There is a tiny window next to the door. Pinned to the door is a clutter of notes all written in different hands: phone numbers, exclamations, messages like broken haikus. Next to them hangs an old canvas backpack and a machete in its sheath. Above them a sheet of foolscap, on which is written in biro: 'It was a dream and it wasn't a dream' and a doodle of something that looks like a surprised teddy bear. Stuck on the foolscap is a pink Post-It note, on which is scribbled: '18 April: honourable, fair, pugnacious, emotionally unstable' — *The Secret Language of Birthdays*. Light filters through the window. Every revealed object takes on a rich and faded appearance. A dilapidated green Genoa armchair. Behind it, hanging on the wall, angled toward the door, a mirror, round with scalloped edges. Its double faces it. A coffee table beside the chair, scarred and marked with cigarette burns. On the table an ashtray, a stack of books, a small green tin, a china cup, a china teapot, a single-burner gas ring, a pack of index cards each crossed with a few scribbled words, some basic bookbinding tools and a simple candelabra with four arms. Opposite the Genoa an upright timber chair, once white. Beside the chair, a dented kerosene heater flickering blue flame. A cleared space on the bookshelves holds a small CD player and speakers. Stashed beside it, a bottle of water, a small black notebook, a red fountain pen and a bottle of black ink.

In the margins of her books, Acker writes new texts subverting or destroying what she has been reading, fragments scattered across innumerable pages in many volumes that continually reconfigure themselves at the back of her mind, sometimes cohering in the liminal space of her dreams. When she re-reads the books on her shelves, the books she has kept, she reads to decode her own marginalia.

She once made a novel out of three other books, ripped up Dickens and maybe Bataille. She can't fucking remember anymore, and doesn't much care. Maybe it was a dead end. Or maybe when a woman fucks with literature, exposing its insides full of worms and tumours and evidence of violence, it's just . . .

She always has to pause for a moment here. What was the word? She's losing her memory in bits and pieces, all the time. Experimental. Acker laughs every time she thinks of the Australian university that kept her books in a locked cabinet and only allowed them out on surrender of ID. And you could only read them there and then.

Sitting next to the cabinet full of horrors.

By the door of her office is a stack of books that are no longer of interest. Acker discards more books than she keeps, dumping them in the rusting yellow skip in the carpark where the Emporium staff stack their empty cardboard boxes. Sometimes, just for fun, she buys a copy of Joyce's *Ulysses* just so she can throw it away. The Fat Elvis of literature, using the labyrinth of his psychosis to build a labyrinth, obsessed with the bifiurcations of his own interior life and putting 'yes' into the mouths of women. If Lucia Joyce came to see me with her stories of loss and claustrophobia, she often thinks, I would listen carefully for as long as it took. And then say quietly, Tell me more about your dad.

The burning cigarette has gone out. The tarot pack that Acker made for herself out of the index cards has ten cards laid out for reading. They are tarot without pictures on each of which Acker has written the name of an image: the Tower, the Queen of Swords, the Fool. A dozen of the cards have the names of images that have never existed in any tarot, major arcana that Acker has herself devised: the Wound, the Fuckwit, Approaching Rain, the Rockslide, the Bag Lady, Lantana. Many others have been renamed. Her minor arcana are Stones, Lightning, Seeds, Scars. Her royal suits are Buddhas, Bodhisattvas, Arhats.

The Fool sits lost in thought. In speaking with others she creates her life (Six Scars). She thinks of loss but does not know what has disappeared (the Tower). Because of this, she does not know what her mistakes were either (the Blind Beggar). Or what sins she may have committed (the Bloody Knife). She has visions but does not always know which are true and which are false (the Schizophrenic). She needs insight (Three of Stones) but knows that she will never receive the great insight she desires (Null Lightning). Something strange and invisible nears (Approaching Rain). Whatever it is, it will have to be enough (the Dead River). No Buddhas appear.

In the beginning, after she came through the Round Window and had only writing to give her being, before she started dismembering books, Acker planned to write a dictionary of invented ideas, a failed attempt to short-circuit her thinking.

Fictional Rendering. (n.) What other people call 'real life'

Oneiric Sedimentation. (n.) What other people call 'thinking'

A dictionary, an attempt to name the Ten

Thousand Things. Should she order them alphabetically or, like a thesaurus, plot them around some conceptual hub, breaking the universe down into a handful of wondrous ideas: time, volition, change, matter?

In the end it became The Dictionary of Three Things.

—

Acker leaves the café with a grateful nod to the owner who always looks at her as though she were a stranger from a very distant part of her life that she is only now starting to remember. A hooded figure trudges slowly along the village street through the slow dissolving fog, knuckling its face and heading for the patch of waste ground half a block down where all the deals are hatched and the pot dispersed; someone who has slept in a car now grabbing at the corner of the day, a day of bruises and hurried deals.

Back in the office, Acker jabs the remote at the CD player. It cycles continually through the piano music of Philip Glass. Acker takes her notebook and pen and rolls another cigarette as she sits back in the Genoa and wonders what the passing of the day will bring to the street and what could happen that might still be prevented if she only knew how to speak the words to make it so.

One of the consequences of experiencing catastrophe is that you start to see ghosts everywhere. As the weeks and months pass, the world becomes increasingly populated by them, each image emanating distorted copies of itself, sometimes with alarming clarity and intensity. These apparitions appear without warning, fused to tiny moments in the world. It's as if time is able to turn back on itself like a Möbius strip and things that have a likeness, or a similar structure or interiority, melt together forming a seamless mirror-like surface.

Acker feels like a displaced person in a weird country where spectres familiarly walk the streets and opening a door can take you anywhere across time into landscapes so strange and unexpected that one would need a second language to describe them.

Or perhaps that's how fucked up I am, she thinks. I see people who aren't there.

Acker gulps her coffee, uncaps her pen and starts to write a description of the map that will take her where she needs to go. As she writes, Acker tries to dovetail the things that make up a day's temperament, the base elements of the life of the street and all its complex and unpredictable influences so that one day, perhaps sooner than she can know, she can write the story of the day, of the street's temper, before it happens, and in fact use her notebook — itself an influence that needs to be accounted for in order to be able to describe the day — to write so that she will never need to leave her office, but only inscribe in her notebook the shape of the mirror in which she can see all things beyond it.

The problem, as she sees it, (humming along to 'Metamorphosis Five') is all the intentions and languages of our forgotten and discarded selves, the ones that follow us around and create the atmospheres of our days, gathering them around us like old blankets. In Acker's scrutiny of those who wait outside her dingy office behind the village street, who sit in the upright chair opposite and watch themselves in the mirror above her head, and in her observations of the crowded life of the village, one thing is clear to her: Nobody is a bare unity. Everybody comes in sheaves. Each living soul waiting at her door appears with a host of invisible others in train, dumb spectres trying to find ways to speak, to invent versions of language, each of them obscured, eroded and entombed by the others. They appear in their scores and hundreds, paper-thin they seem, crowded as if in a finite space beyond whose edges they would disappear. Even the grieving mother is a crowd, a gathering of all the mothers she could have been to all the children who didn't grow up.

At such times, Acker is acutely conscious of both a person's absence and their presence, as though there were a template of them cut out of space and time, a kind of shadow in her mind that projects itself onto a world she is both violently present in and oddly dislocated from. And to speak to this throughout the day, and often into the night, when all the ghosts and spectres of the disowned selves of others come crowding in on her, seeking an end — as if there were places in Australia where all the unwept griefs could go to be transfigured into something as prosaic and useful as shoes — Acker has become fluent in a kind of dream language, a ramshackle parade of syntax. Behind the use of language, she says to herself, is an unending wish, a wish that we could have a faultless exchange of our murderous interior landscapes. But language is a sleight of hand that both reveals and hides the existence of the unspeakable; that reminds us there are things about ourselves we can never know, that knowing is endless and uncageable, and to understand each other is an approximation of a dream.

Acker looks into the mirror above the door and lets herself know the score: you ask me a question,

I give you a broken bone; you wonder aloud, I present you with a scorched rag. This is how we will talk, Acker. You will offer me your unthinking words and I will carefully select an object from my heap of random wreckage. Eventually, I will have a vocabulary of distraught images that I will invest with magical properties. Here is a picture of an eyeball. Not to tell you that there is something to be seen but to say that the sky never really sleeps, that ordinary looking is a kind of blindness, that light is not the same everywhere.

When alone in her office, and not cutting up books or writing, Acker sits and looks at her mind. She is not certain what she is looking at it with, but has slowly become convinced that who she thought was looking was just a trace, a bare outline of herself that no one had ever filled in, something nominal, something said to be her, but said only. And what is looking at the mind is an aspect of her mind not previously noted, like the mirror's capacity for reflection, a capacity not located in anything, that is of no concrete agent or place but real and active nonetheless.

Acker has to sit and let something of herself disappear a little. She is always amazed to find her thoughts, or the thing she has privileged as thought, chugging away apparently without any motive or intention on her part. And then slowly, the politics of thinking begins to unreel, to become apparent, as if what would be revealed in them is a picture of her face unrecognisable to her. It is like walking into my office, she thinks, and finding someone else sitting in it, someone to all purposes myself, but of whom I know nothing of at all, while they know everything about me, even the things I have forgotten or have had burned away. When she looks ruefully at her act of looking, Acker's reassertion of herself blows itself out like a candle flame, leaving no sign of its absence, not even a trace of smoke.

There are many ways to destroy a novel, Acker has found. And it's satisfying to carry on old habits, to show herself that while her memory is becoming increasingly threadbare, as if bits of her were continually flaking off, writing still makes sense, still helps her put what is left of herself together. In the evenings, by candlelight, using knife, glue and pen Acker dismembers books, tears out their insides and then reconstructs them, revealing their bizarre and occasionally subversive natures, cutting the bindings of polite and linear form. Or perhaps she is just someone who thinks a novel is something of a butcher's shop and should look like one. And as she sits late into the night, by the flare of candles, eviscerating another book, she remembers to clearly ascertain what it is she is disemboweling; the self-sufficient thing assuming an essential reality. Acker cuts and binds. Dismembers and glues. She slices open a children's book and interleaves it with the gutted copy of some literary great that lies on the table like a frog pinned out in a laboratory.

It is the children's picture books that are the most disturbing. She cannot make sense of them, and cannot understand why she cannot make sense of them. It is like flicking through images from Goya redrawn by Walt Disney. Acker struggles to bring out their bizarre nature, a nature that seems to her to be as strange as the heads of grotesque insects set in the welkin. Acker imagines projects where the canonical texts of English literature are illustrated by pictures of animals with the eyelashes of starlets, or cars and trucks with chubby-cheeked smiles and cheeky winks. Any way to fuck with them a bit. Or even better, she thinks, yes even better, would be to read them in the voice of the Nmbngee.

Acker stands and searches briefly through her shelves, finger-tipping along the ordered spines. She pulls out Amos Tutuola's *My Life in the Bush of Ghosts* and Alexis Wright's *Plains of Promise* and begins to trawl her way through the cryptic utterances of her own marginalia, struggling to remember the line of her thought, the place where thought and reverie took her, following disintegrating threads back into the past.

—

And deep into the night, the door firmly shut against the unimaginable happenings on the street, of which more later, Acker drags at her cigarette and on the endpaper of another book, some author's most cherished creation whose title we cannot quite see, plots its physical destruction in brief cryptic notes.

To write is to read. To write is to find the way in. The difference between writing what is true and what is false lies in never pretending that you are writing of others, of some separately existing external world. Acker creates in her writing her own awareness, a knowledge of herself that is contiguous with the surface of the world. She uses her writing for herself to remember her self. She causes her self to fold back on itself, *pli selon pli*. Whatever I write writes me. I am reading this with you, she wants to say to her reader, discovering what I am writing. We do this to each other, with each other. There isn't any other way it can work. If you think that you can read a book, without the book reading you, I don't know what to say to you.

But this is all before us. The morning light is gaining a granular coherence, is inviting itself in through the single window. Acker writes and writes.

—

Up on the street, as the morning passes, demands are being made that become calls sent out like radio signals. Acker stands and puts on her jacket, checks tobacco, lighter, wallet, kills the CD player just as it is about to run into Glass's 'Mad Rush', and steps out into the transparent day. She walks the few paces up the alleyway to the main street of the village and leaning on one shoulder at the alleyway entrance, rolls a cigarette and watches, for a few moments, the street parade.

The sun breaks out and bright angled shadows, luminous, chop their way along the street. And through the sheet of sunlight hanging behind the village, Acker sees the black rain over Blue Knob like a cloud of ink under a sky that is a tower of light.

It's true that the village street — that probably has more weird and occult events take place on it than any other street in the country — has a temperament that changes according to a complex series of causes that Acker has yet to map but that she has become adept at attuning herself to. It has always seemed to Acker that the village is inhabited by as many spirits as human beings, where people appear and disappear like bubbles and others seem to have the heads of animals, and clouds are writing messages in an arcane language in the sky. In Elizabethan London, St Paul's Cathedral was a marketplace filled with merchants, dealers, cutpurses, yokels, spies, poets, prostitutes, gang bosses, beggars, cripples and priests. And when she read about this babbling thoroughfare in one of her now-dismembered books Acker laughed out loud and immediately thought of the village on a crowded Sunday morning, the sky steepled with raincloud gathering from behind the shadow of Blue Knob, where those who are said to be beautiful turn into versions of Quasimodo and haunt the shadows at night, and the ugly and humiliated find themselves transforming into the children they never had the chance to become.

And from the 'outside', as Acker thinks of it, she can sometimes feel and hear, as if at a great distance, vast structures slowly collapsing, the sounds of the world coming apart. It is most likely just the festering corpse of capitalism, she says to herself, still twitching like a whale on a beach with neo-fascists picking over the carcass, shrieking like roosters under a sky full of predators.

The gaudy antique shopfronts are packed together like painted boxes. Scattered along the footpaths are clusters of old couches and chairs, encampments of activists, smokers, guitarists, fortune tellers and buskers, children counting shared coins, chess players and dealers doing business, all the thousand forums of turbulent confederation jostling for room. The sun bleaches the street that is already filling with dozens of sunburned backpackers with their blank drifting gaze, living in circuits, following a path like a rut in time, crossing and re-crossing borders, a kind of indeterminate nation of the floating world. They are bussed in from the coast like cattle, to look at the weirdos and maybe score a bag of pot.

Acker observes the scene unreel before her, and at the same time she seems to be watching it from above, following all the activity down the length of the crowded street, a mild and momentary out-of-body experience that bothers her from time to time, like an old injury. The locals in their many genders and accents and languages, their post-punk courtesies, erratic friendliness and slum-circus clothing, talk of the rain and of each other, making knots on the footpaths around which the tourists squeeze themselves. A few wet dogs quest around. Across the road outside the post office a couple of squabbling French backpackers screaming of *mérde* throw clothes out of a campervan onto the footpath. A group of Pommy boys, bare-chested and loud, swagger line abreast toward the laneway and its knot of young dealers, tattooed and vigilant, where they will become suddenly mute or there will be the makings of a fight. Acker watches them a moment longer. Mute. A young couple, city-dressed, fresh out of their car, sun-glassed and water-bottled, with a baby dolled up in a stroller, peer uncertainly into the window of the apothecary. There is a continually unfolding scrimmage outside the doors of the Emporium, with people entering empty-handed and hurriedly, then leaving shopping-bagged and slowly. At the centre of this scrimmage paths collide; people caught by greetings stopping mid-stride, standing awkwardly by the waiting dogs leashed to the seat where the busker with the harp sits and plays Irish dances and the backpackers queue for the ATM. Children thread rapidly and expertly through the shifting crowd, calling to each other.

And next door, in the village pharmacy, the wounded and damaged gather for their complex cocktails of medication to dissolve the pain in their bones or in the structure of their minds, each package dispensed to them with a neat dignity and the knowledge that there is no one who seeks to have their lives contained within a box of pills, to be driven into a pharmacy as if into a butcher's shop where you are handed your own entrails with a price tag.

The village is like a child's constructed town made of books and kitchen pots and boxes and bits of junk and a few coloured blocks that has been abandoned to dust and time and then redis-covered and repainted by someone on a long acid trip, obsessed with trees, snakes, Buddhas, pri-meval forests and skies saturated with angels, this Sunday, yes it is Sunday, and market day, where the village is as crowded as it can be and the sun-light luminous and yellow makes everything ring like a bell.

> Stained-glass apperception (n.) The
> moment when you feel illuminated by your
> knowledge of the world's ruin

The night Acker turned up, an explosive storm tore in from behind the Rocks, snapped mature gum trees in half, created chasms metres deep where roads and watercourses crossed and then disappeared into the northeast, dissolving into the sea. At dawn the sky was clear and pale, already abraded a little by the hint of the next storm brewing south of west like smoke from a distant factory. To Acker's right the Rocks had loomed like monks, and she began to slowly push her way down the steep hillside through the briars of lantana that cracked like the bones of birds and which toward the road she could see thrown like a piece of string across the valley floor. The road was littered with smashed branches and shredded leaves as if a barrage of artillery airbursts had exploded in the crowns of the trees. The silence was eerie as though she was standing inside an empty glass. Acker had felt as though she was trying to re-enter a life she had once imagined, perhaps in her writing somewhere, believing that she could find a doorway to such a thing, believing that such a thing could even exist, as though she could convince herself that she was standing on that threshold. But however much you tell yourself that you can see the image of your future, the flood of causality relentlessly bursts the frame of time.

And yet in the past, it now seemed to her, she had inhabited a kind of reflexive image as though she existed within a mirror, and knew she was within a mirror, without being able to see herself. This is what her previous life seemed to be, a life in which she walked among her friends like a character in her own novels — riven with anxiety, scarified by desire, traumatised by the rigid violent gendering of the world — but happy in her way, preoccupied with her own preoccupation, working industriously enough at whatever job it was she had a few days a week and the rest of the time just as industriously writing, hacking through the thickets of her own thought, every book she finished a pirate ship sent out into the world.

And now, in this illuminated present in which she lives and writes, something within her has completely revolved, as if grinding on a pivot, like a giant iron key turning over once in a lock. And in doing so it made enough noise to wake every ghost, spectre and haunted freak within a hundred miles. And they all came and sat outside her door.

Acker leans against the wall at the alley's narrow entrance, toying absently with an unlit cigarette.

She is always observing others without them observing her. A tensile lenticular shell, like the eye of the hatched cicada. The Acker who speaks is a ghost, solitary, wry, fascinated by the surface of things, by blistered paint, guttered rainwater, skin, tears. Acker sighs and squints into the sunlight. All these people I'm watching, all other, are not really wholly other and I can prove it. She pockets the cigarette and begins a long tour of the street.

The village is probably the only place in the world where one could actually be the resurrected Kathy Acker and get away with it. And perhaps that's Poly Styrene too sitting on the bench in the bus shelter by the park and grinning at the passers-by, flashing her x-ray vision. Acker and Poly nod at each other sometimes, but it always seems as though there is a wall of glass between them that they cannot break. We are like two secret agents in Berlin, thinks Acker, each on her own mysterious mission.

And maybe Elvis is here as well, fat and bald, sitting behind Poly in the little park with the war memorial, drinking Jim Beam and telling the Kooris, who gather there around the never-ending campfire, long boring stories of the time he joined the army and how he got an Elvis impersonator to double for him and finally got out from under the thumb of Colonel Tom. The Kooris know he's lying, but they are used to whitefellahs' lies and spotted this ancient fool as a fraud a mile away. Acker nods to the Auntie who likes to chat to her sometimes in the café, checking up on her, just in case. She yells a greeting and her relatives laugh and wave. Acker smiles, throws an arm up and crosses the road. The marble plinth in the park is filled on every side with the incised names of the war dead, so many for such a little village where it has always seemed to Acker that the dead out-number the living.

Though let it not be thought that Acker has forgotten the murdered children. Far from it. In fact she is hot on the trail, tracing in her mind Australia's bloody history of lost, imprisoned and murdered children, the history of Australia as a gulag to which terrified children are condemned: the Stolen Generations, kidnapped in their tens of thousands; the children who grew up and called themselves the Forgotten, half a million thrown into institutional care and routinely brutalised as part of a policy of benevolence; the detention camps for asylum seekers where children are raped and abused and hurt themselves so they can remember they are alive, and people burn themselves to death just to break the silence in which they have been immured.

In this country, the murder of children has its own etiology, a sanctioning scored so deeply into Australian life that violence flows along well-worn gutters overwhelming the same people, over and over.

But following the dead is not a straightforward matter, even for one who apparently now has a gift for it.

The rain has cleared. The sky is brimming blue, and the black cloud over Blue Knob has risen up like a ghost and vanished into the upper air. Hands in pockets, Acker kicks across the street toward the Sunday markets, laid out among the buildings of the old primary school, now the studios, workshops and offices of the community centre. It is Sunday and market day. The village has sprouted a bewildering variety of tiny unsanctioned street stalls that spill over the worn disordered footpaths all the way down to the market site proper. A beatbox pumps out trance music. There are tables full of hats, oranges, machetes and saws, bush foods, handmade jewellery, flowers, Buddhas, children's toys, rainforest plants, cut herbs, books, and jars of jam. Children sell handmade cards and boxes of plastic dinosaurs at fifty cents a pop. The children keep some money for ice cream and mandarins and give the rest to Sea Shepherd. The jams are a way of rescuing ancient recipes and cementing a relationship between two small farms and three generations of women and saying fuck you to Centrelink. The rainforest plants are grown in a preschool as part of a drawing project three metres wide called 'Why aren't there enough trees?'.

It is here at the market that Acker goes to talk to the Beautiful Girl, the woman she has fallen in love with, to wonder how that happened and why it happened now. It may well be, Acker thought the previous night, sitting in the office, the candle flames steady, strange clatterings and chitterings on the roof, it may be that I just want to stand in front of something good. And so, in the revealing of her deeply catastrophic existence, Acker is made happy.

The Beautiful Girl is selling native plants: grevilleas, banksias, callistemons, some violets and daisies. Acker feels a kind of brittle persona cohering as she casually flips a hand in greeting and crouches to touch the bloom on a flowering grevillea.

Oh, says the Beautiful Girl, as though Acker had alighted on a shared happiness.

Of course it's the unsayable that Acker immediately becomes aware of, as she looks upward into that radiant smile. In the pause, over the soft murmur of the market's hubbub the Beautiful Girl says, How was your week, Acker?

Even a psychopomp has to earn a crust, to moonlight a little. But when you spend those crust-earning hours neck deep in the shame, the violence and the schizophrenia of ordinary life, mundane conversation can routinely fail you, even with someone you love.

Acker can only answer with a private joke. (After all, she thinks much later, what could I have said? Well at the moment I'm thinking of the dead children I have to find, and yesterday there was the incident with the psychotic writer and his magic ball of string and the night before that I kicked a well-known creep in the balls and threw him off the bridge into the creek. I need an offsider, she thinks, a porkpie hat wearing, wise-cracking muscleman, even more tormented than me, more ruthless, more philosophical.)

I looked at the stars.

And ate nightmares? says the Beautiful Girl smiling, misquoting Acker back to herself.

Yes, says Acker's brittle persona, violent and unworkable, unsuited to her thought. And when things got weird (holding up the grevillea) I planted some trees.

The Beautiful Girl smiles back at her. It's all copacetic, she says.

Acker feels like her heart is smiling. That's why I love her, she thinks. Who else would take the trouble to read my books and quote the signature phrase of a fucked-up fictional PI just to cheer me up?

Acker pays for the grevillea and leaves it with the Beautiful Girl while she wanders off through the market, looking for clues, reminders, seren-dipities, knowing that at the end she will be gifted a tree.

The grass is covered with yellow leaves from the fig trees and camphors that once shaded children at lunchtimes. The black soil shows through like the worn spots on an old carpet. The market is a dense clutter of stalls, marquees, converted campers and purpose-built trailers that unfold like origami, all packed under the shade of the trees and eaves of the building: the food vendors' ancient vans, painted like vardos, that dispense pizza or samosas or pancakes seemingly without money being exchanged; the bread stall where everyone waits patient as trees while the baker describes in detail to every curious customer the alchemy of sourdough baking in a woodfired oven, outdoors at 4 am; the stall where the garden vegetables are so ridiculously cheap that one feels anxious about buying them, as though one were engaging in an act of theft. At the coffee cart the espresso machine hisses like a small dragon turning in its sleep, and behind boxes of LPs a young man in sunnies and a trilby rocks back in his camping chair, lights up a joint, and reads the lyric sheet to *Sandinista!*

People are gathering by the gate, wandering through in twos and threes in the passing clouds of sunlight: lovers, fingers lightly entangled; old friends making arrangements for lunch; family members hurriedly sharing gossip and useful household information; the sunburned back-packer girls all in singlets and shorts and briefly rose gold in the patches of sun, laughing at secret shared jokes; the elderly woman from out west touring the village with her reluctant husband (she has some inkling of a life that might still be infected with a little joy); a few stoned surfers blown in from the coast looking for entertainment to fill the dragging day. Gangs of children, pulled together by a kind of gravity, mill around, are struck by bright ideas and disperse like meteors.

Everything is sleepy as though just emerging from a vague early morning dream. The children don't care, but the adults chat quietly as though they are in church, as though aware that they are still bridging the distance between waking and sleeping and their words may carry a strange weight.

The rounded leaves of the fig trees are lit up despite the passing cloud, and shelter fruit doves like green flames. The sky is a winter blue like faded cloth, the sun a bright glinting shard that makes the shadows seem deeper, harbouring portents and signs. Up on the little market stage a woman is playing guitar and singing quietly, barely loud enough to be heard, as though she is far away, or in another room, or Acker herself is floating just beneath the surface of water. The guitarist sometimes misses her notes that tumble over each other like stairs collapsing down a hillside.

Her voice carries something about dreams and broken hearts.

No one sings about justice anymore, Acker thinks.

Acker drifts through the market — pauses in mid-step while a couple of two year olds cross her path hand in hand, snickering — keeps drifting. She finds a seat in the shade by a little chai stall and slowly drinks a pot of tea. The tree drops a tiny green spider onto her sleeve. A preschool-aged child in a crown, Supergirl t-shirt and tutu and clutching a golden wand adorned with a glitter-pasted star skids to a halt by Acker's table, stands for a second, arms akimbo, frowning, zaps Acker and speeds away victorious.

If Acker couldn't bear the spears in her heart there'd be no point doing this job. She watches the child disappear into the crowd and thinks of all the children who once started their mornings kitting themselves up with a magic wand and their favourite dress-ups, blasting everyone with spells of transformation and who, before the sun had gone down, ended up dead on a living room floor because their father wanted to punish their mother.

Acker, an hour later; same table, new pot of tea. Sometimes her days are like lungfuls of clean air, infused with a dreaming quality as if the whole day were blue, all perceptions knitted together, all surfaces contiguous. It is as if everything is a transparent shadow of something else.

The rain will later sweep in black sheets across the valley and the hills behind Blue Knob will become vast pale silhouettes, the valleys of air between them filled and mapped by pointillist mist, opening up a perception of vast distance, just as the Magellanic Clouds give the illusion of human perspective to the flat night sky.

The market is crowded now. Bustling, noisy. A reggae band is pumping out heavy beats from the stage. Acker wanders again searching now for books, because books are always clues, books are always a key. Inviolable rule of book hunting: Nothing is ever too tattered, threadbare or humble to look at.

Parked in the middle of the winding ramshackle trail of market stalls, in the deep shade of one of the figs is an old Toyota LiteAce van, apparently unattended, doors wide open on all sides, from which appear to have spilled piles of ancient suitcases. Laid out on the grass like the discarded luggage of wartime evacuees, in their open mouths are arranged a strange and chaotic variety of objects: pamphlets from the 1950s about Scouting; threadbare hand-embroidered tablecloths; a doll with a porcelain head and papery Edwardian clothes; pen-knives; a rare John Coltrane LP; a dusty crystal ball; a pair of alligator-skin boots hazed with scratches; a scarred walking stick with a brass animal's head; an almanac of tides and navigational data; a set of ancient gold-embossed encyclopaedias missing X–Z; a stack of dog-eared Australian literary journals; foxed volumes of astrology all scattered among rags of antique clothing, comics, postcards and collections of tea-spoons and barbed wire.

Well, fuck me, says Acker. She picks up a bat-tered hardback edition of *My Mother: Demonology* that lies upside down between an ancient hand-axe and what appears to be an ornate glass bong. Jesus, the places where one's wrung-out heart turns up. I barely remember writing this. On the book's yellowing flyleaf is a scribbled signa-ture like that of a child. God, what was I on? On second thoughts, she thinks turning the page, perhaps I really was that innocent. But when Acker reads, 'Each door half-opened to unex-pected violence' something stirs within her, as disorienting as if she were hallucinating bats, and she puts the book down.

Everything Acker ever wrote in that weird and antique and prescient life, life of a different velocity and engineering, has a shape that has migrated into this collapsed and splintered version of reality, in this landscape called Australia, at the end of the world, living among the ruins of what was a complex and sophisticated Indigenous culture, laid to waste by the colonisers in apocalyptic fervour in ways we have not yet begun to encompass.

Acker steps out of the shade, turns, and glances back at the little van and its circle of suitcase middens, as something strange and momentary and unsettling seems to shake the air, the very line between Acker's imagined present and the remnants of the disordered past.

There is very little in this bizarre and unknowable world that is not permeated with some kind of suffering. And now, at the market under the winter sun in the forgotten country village, Acker is suddenly swollen by an intense kind of looking, as though she has momentarily acquired a kind of telescopic clarity of vision, unencumbered with the penumbras of meaning we graft onto the world. Acker sees herself, as though watching from a great distance, not ambling through a village market but living through the aftermath of an apocalypse where we trade in terminally ruptured meaning, in broken objects of memory and desire, a few people flogging off the leavings of whatever it is that comprises daily life, each item loaded with some kind of unmeasurable significance: the porcelain doll; the reptile-skinned boots; the weird curios; the book with its alien signature telling of unimaginable times and places long gone and nearly uninterpretable, like folktales from a culture of dreams and night terrors, gathering whatever shattered meaning and memory it still possesses into a profusion of mythic and broken items.

In marginal spaces where things continually fray around the edges and identities corrode before our eyes, perhaps it's possible to see, in the charade of the normal, the shimmer of unreality. Maybe, Acker thinks, if we live where corrosion, age and dying are in the nature of things, where memory looks more like the surface of a sheet of rusted tin than a streamlined event, the way that things end seems more believable, the apocalypse less apocalyptic, so to speak, and more particular. Here we are, she says to herself — not for the first time — here we are, never really sure that we're not stuck in some sort of Tibetan *bardo*, the In-Between, where you wander for forty-nine days, or a week, or ten years, or an aeon, stuck outside time like an insect buzzing against a pane of glass. For a second Acker's mind looks back toward the entrance to this existence and is seized by a panic that bends her spine and almost drives her to her knees.

It's worse than being dead, she thinks. It's *as if* I were dead. Fuck.

Acker pulls herself together. Straightens up. Takes a breath. Okay, I'm on it. She makes a bee-line for her little office and on the way collects her grevillea from the Beautiful Girl, she so pleased for her. Acker's heart seems to fill her chest as they part.

—

Acker grabs her backpack off the back of the door, drops into it water bottle, ink, notebook, pen, throws it over one shoulder, unhooks the machete and clips it to her belt and runs down to the carpark. The ignition of the F100 lurches, fires, and the engine grumbles like a subwoofer. The carpark is filling with sedans and campervans and Acker eases the truck past the family groups unpacking themselves and the clusters of backpackers sorting through the disorder of their vans and swings out into the street.

The truck crawls through the Elizabethan throng as the mixtape kicks in and Nina Simone sings of Time. Through Acker's windscreen the crowded street seems faded and faraway like an image in a crystal ball all shadows and dreamy revelation, while glancing either right or left is like looking into the windows of a passing train where in rapid succession — so fast it is as if they are overlaid on one another — one sees a raised arm, an open mouth, a running child, splintered light.

The village is so filled with people and animals that it seems that the strip of sky fixed to the length of the street must also be crowded with traffic, with crows, king parrots, swallows, raptors and other things moving too fast to register on the cognition, and then Acker is through and guns the truck past the police station and the hospital, past the narrow side street that runs down to the paddocks where it is said the massacres of the Widjabul took place, and heads out of town toward the turn-off by the Rocks, shaking off the residue of the village as a dog shakes off water.

The Rocks are colossal above Acker's truck as it grinds past them, blundering over potholes. A few tags have tried to stick to them over the decades, names the first squatters tried on, stamping everything with a label: Cathedral Rock; the Thimble; the Needles. Acker has always thought of Cathedral Rock as a Niobe, arms raised frozen in grief for her slain children. The Thimble is obviously a *stupa* she thinks, watching composed over Niobe, an immovable witness to her unending sorrow. The Needles are like the sheer wall of a great blasted crater, the remnant of a fireball that turned rock to glass before evaporating into a white limitless sky leaving a vast carbonised shell, eventually colonised by the great forests.

In magnitudes of scale, thinks Acker, a human being is no more than a hop-o-my-thumb. I'm looking into time and I can't see the bottom. It is as if something outside of human experience has arisen out of the earth or descended from the sky through the curtains of rain.

Acker turns off the bitumen and takes the truck up a narrow dirt road into shadow. A few kilometres rattle by. She parks under a clutch of flooded gums, kills the engine, jumps out of the cabin. She belts her leather jacket around her waist, and speculatively eyes the wall of lantana, already grown back since she was last here. The cicadas shriek in synchrony and the sound seems to rise out of the lantana in waves. The Rocks are off to Acker's left and seem to have moved closer together, clustered as if concealing something from her gaze, or arranging themselves for what is to come, like a chorus in a Greek play.

Acker adjusts her backpack, hefts the machete and begins to hack her way up the slope, tunneling through the lantana. Fucking stuff. I'm going to spend the rest of time cutting my way through lantana. Shattering the brittle canes of lantana leaves a cross-hatching of red scratches on her bare arms from wrist to elbow. They will sting a little with sweat, and blood and sweat will smear across her tattoos. The clear ring of the machete against the lantana is like the chiming of a length of tiny cracked bells. There is a noise like cloth tearing as the wet lantana collapses.

From the clearing at the top of the hill Acker can see a scattering of rooftops like jewellery boxes among the trees. Sounds reach her like chimes. Laughter. The knocking of a hammer. Shout of a child. A dove calls, popping out a soft carillon somewhere deep in the forest.

Acker sits under the gaunt twisted sally wattle that shades the little clearing, wipes the sweat off her face with her t-shirt, checks herself for ticks, pulls off her boots, tugs a couple of leeches off an ankle and flicks them into the bush. A few lizards scoot about the scuffy yellow grass knotted to the rhyolite. The village is concealed by the curve of the ridge opposite, but she can feel it there like a weight in a net. Across a kilometre of air, the Rocks wait.

She takes the water bottle out of her backpack, along with her notebook and fountain pen. The drone-like buzzing of the cicadas comes and goes with the breaking through of the sun, so that it seems as though the sunlight itself is vibrating like a clockwork cello.

Acker writes, trying to squeeze her mind

through a narrow pipe, until every object she can see haemorrhages its own ghost. The landscapes of the dead draw nearer and nearer, heavier and heavier, sinking toward her like a rain of stones. The way in is always through some horrible bullshit narrative, some travail of suffering. In this case it will be the cage and slavery and then an escape she will engineer on a dim shore, the sky saturated with ash, a city burned to cinders. She knows what she will have to become, the shape she will have to assume, the ruthless transformation that will gut her like a fish, her mind torn up like someone with lycanthropy, her body undergoing a kind of mutilated transformation like the raped child who feels their insides are falling out.

You'll be 'Dog', she thinks, and sighs just a little, ruefully. You are always 'Dog'. And wherever she arises, 'Dog' always works whatever her appearance, attaching itself to her as naturally as a shadow, and mute as one too, as if writers at the moment of transformation into a writer become incapable of speech. And it helps her to maintain her intention too. Helpful, friendly, alert.

Okay, she thinks. I know where they are. And lays aside her notebook and fountain pen, puts on her jacket to protect herself a little from the rain that will come in during the afternoon, takes a long drink of water, leans back against the trunk of the sally wattle and waits. The Rocks take up their stance of mourning. Acker comforts herself by imagining that the Nmbngee becomes attentive.

Transformation, said Proust at the very beginning of his search for lost time, is like a kind of reincarnation, like being the subject of a book one is reading and then becoming separate from that book by way of passing through a zone of unintelligibility. For Acker it is much more precise.

The light in the valley, the Rocks shadowing the edge of her vision, shimmers like a mirage, begins to waver like water vapour, then flares like a blizzard of sparks. Acker's conscious awareness seems to spasm like the flame of a guttering candle. Every sense, every cognition, floods with white, then glows red, plunges into a pitch black void and finally, with a dense flicker of transparent light, precipitates her with a rush of terror into new senses. Memories are blown through her like a storm of leaves. They dissolve into a host of shadows like bats filling the sky at dusk. Everything has the sticky, claustrophobic texture of a dream. Fear grips her, rises like a fish and punctures the dream's surface. Waking, she is always waking.

||

Asky like a bloodstain. A wind that is like the ragged voices of the grieving. Tenuous sheets of light, weightless, unjunctured, suddenly a landscape. The cage she anticipated, the voyage and the escape, have somehow already happened, like a dream in which you know you have to walk a certain road, so you already have, as though it were inside you, as though the experience and the memory of it arose simultaneously. An ocean hisses behind her and out beyond the convulsion of waves, it looks like multitudes are drowning.

Twilight rushes in and collapses into a flat shattered print of speckled light, a chopped space of stars. There is a sliver of moon. A hard metallic shriek scores a line through the air. A weird liquefied green light shudders high above, as though the apocalyptic shadows of ghouls and spectres of another world are projected onto a transparent curtain.

The stars vanish. A devastated landscape flickers like the light from distant storms. Sometimes there is a dry stony road and sometimes not. There is no sun, only a half-light that seems to come from everywhere. Dog walks across a plain the colour of rust, into a landscape that will become eerily familiar, like the country of Widjabul turned inside out, its features distended, a paddock becoming a burning desert, a village street an incinerated city, a termite mound a labyrinth, sunlight a rain of ash.

In an empty landscape without shadows, little hovels of rags and sheets of paper appear in their millions, incised out of the flat light, packed together like tents in a refugee camp or stacked like *favelas* and they reach from horizon to horizon. The light around them has turned sepia as though it descended long ago and has remained, slowly discolouring. There is a black circle in an ochre sky, its face scored with lines as if from an old scourging, and a deadly hum in the air.

The land is both empty and replete with the murdered dead and glimmers with etiolated images. The dead, their memories atomising, continually disintegrate and reappear. They are unaware of each other, as though to be dead is to be alone neither fortune nor history, consumed by a grief that can never be forgotten. The dead trawl the empty landscape or stand like leeches, waiting, anchored to a corroded fragment of memory, waiting for what they have irrevocably lost, queuing as if to enter some gated world there to be swallowed up in a labyrinth of doors.

As always, the half-disintegrated dreams of the dead flock to Dog like flies, following her like the trail of dust behind a comet, chattering like insects or ravening like hyenas, light failing around them, their fragmentary memories continually dissolving even as they are accreting some new hallucination.

Dog walks through the endless ranks of dwellings, and adjusts herself to the experience of being something of a hallucination herself. Just as how in a dream one never has an awareness of one's outer self but seems to exist only in a skin of perception, so Dog inhabits a liminal state of being, whose shape and appearance will be lit and designated by the glow of the minds of those she seeks. That is, if they haven't yet begun to fall apart; if she can find them.

Dog climbs a long slope up toward a narrow ridge. Soft light, a dull sky. From the top of the ridge, beyond the plain of tents and hovels below, Dog can see the distant sea. Before her a great valley is filled with a dense white fog. Ruined buildings protrude like the stumps of trees.

The light shrinks to a hard point. The fog comes away in rags like bandages being pulled off a burned corpse. Black ruins dissolve to a dark horizon. It is as though the sun had for a moment left its appointed place and lurched toward the earth, scorching a whole arc of the world before wheeling back to its sky. A fine white ash floats, adhering to the air. The city is an endless geo-metric wreckage. Shadows crawl across lines of shallow light.

A grinding sound seems to be emanating from the sky, as if made by some rusting stridula-tion, a sky that sheds a grey light like dirty water. A low clashing sound like a gong being struck by falling metal echoes across the sky in slow crepi-tations. The day passes like the elongated shadow of a presence she cannot see.

A broken road beneath an ember of moon tracks down toward the city. Shadows rise out of the city's ruins and vanish into the starless sky. Far away, over the edge of the world, red light flickers and stabs upward, arcs and falls. A dull glow settles behind a slab of mountain and burns steadily, revealing the belly of the cloud. Silence spreads roots and branches into the sky.

In the darkness, the burned ruins drift. Dog tastes smoke and ash. The children may have already vanished. The space in which the dead know they are dead is very brief, sometimes barely a flash of lightning.

A faint drift of rain falls on an uneven surface of small stones, ash, dirty puddles, pulverised glass, hard burned things. Long shallow pools of water, ash-dusted, bloom with shrouds of pale light.

Brittle silence. Granulated light patterned and printed with the fading rain. Masses of rubble replicated in a machinic template layer on layer, riddled with broken entrances to catacombs. Dog goes in, crawls underground, beneath the suspended veils of ash. Light finds its way in particles, into a calcified labyrinth of collapsed buildings. Random accidental tunnels. The layered archaeology of destruction. Scorched bones and sheaves of paper, burned rags, stone fused to gobbets of glass.

And then, as though time and space are slowly coming apart under some unimaginable pressure, Dog is momentarily outside her own incarnation, and watches herself, small, startling and dirty, emerging from a hole in a wall, watched by the two children. Through a high shattered ceiling floats a cloud of murky light, dense with floating dust.

The children are squatting beside the ashes of a small fire, arms resting on knees. The girl looks at Dog with accusing eyes. Her hair is long, matted, unkempt as though she has been lost for weeks in a wilderness. The boy gives a tiny wet cough and tugs violently at the skin on his pinched, anxious face.

The girl's face grey and white, her gaze like a pressure. Dog closes her eyes. If I look at her I will see in her a wide desolate lake of black water and she will know it.

The girl opens her mouth and speaks with a voice like that of a bird. To Dog her words are a stream of scrambled syllables, as if the scroll in a player piano had been randomly punched with holes scattered across the ordered musical code. As though the first thing to go after the shock of the disintegration of being is language. The girl puts her head down and busies herself by the ashes of the fire. Dog is already a familiar object, one that perhaps has some kind of damaged or disabled function or purpose but that cannot yet be discarded. In an irretrievably broken world where all things are shattered, random apparitions are merely proof that nightmares, dreams and visions are now the foundation stones of reality.

Without looking at Dog the children rebuild

the fire, eat some colourless substance that the girl takes out of a little cloth bag. They fall asleep by the fire, folded together, each wrapped in the arms of the other.

The moon with its corroded face drifts above the pit.

The children are already encased in a stunted ritual: sleeping, waking to gather burned fragments of wood for their fire, eating a little food, sleeping, sleeping, waking again to eat. It is the unimaginable which is growing in them and they are trying to shut it out. There will soon be nothing to eat but dust and ash. The present will become an endless iteration, a succession of days empty of everything but violence, set down one after another like coffins.

While the children sleep Dog returns to the tunnels underground, the radius of cracks beneath the destroyed city, fractured with moonlight. She digs out broken objects as if she were extracting jewels from a mining seam, building a lexicon. She takes what she gathers back to the children and, when the girl wakes, lays them out like hieroglyphics speaking of what is to come, of what is possible. They voice the dreams the girl has woken from. The dream in which she stood on the lip of a vast pit edged by a line of burned trees like twisted wire; the dream in which the bodies of children, trammelled by the discoloured light and disfigured with terrible wounds, lie scattered among the shadows as though flung from a wreck that was drowning in fire.

The girl wakes the boy and speaks to him with a small voice that struggles to hide its distress while it imparts the tone of instruction.

Dog leads the children through the silent ruins, damp with rain. Silhouettes appear out of the air, move as though being pursued, and disappear.

The sky is a flat, even grey. The light, slow and heavy, fringes everything with dissolving shadow. A landscape of ruins on which the weird amoebic dreams of the dead fall, layer upon layer.

The children build a hissing fire behind a rampart of brick. The boy's face is hard and tense. The girl's eyes rest on Dog, briefly transmitting a sense of bewilderment that Dog can feel at the back of her skull. Dog has the strangest sense that she is slipping between nightmare and fairytale and is never sure of the difference.

The children sleep. The sky is filled with a shallow weary light like the last faint pulse from drifting debris, and flickers with distraught images of violence. Dog listens to the voices coming from the landscapes of the dead, worlds as numerous as motes of dust. They all have the same lament, bewildered and confused, as though there were a force without mind or intent at large throughout time and space, a violent and propulsive shadow that lays everything under a malediction. The dead are perpetually vanishing, the world disintegrating around them instantaneous with their experience of it. To be dead is to move through time like a broken machine trying to fulfil some kind of redundant function.

The girl crawls out of her dream-smothered sleep, disentangling herself from the boy. She recollects herself in distinct stages as she wakes, though Dog is never sure whether it is her or the past that falls into place first. The boy shudders in his sleep. He mutters at length, wakes with a start, looks blankly into the sky. He seems to slowly fix himself on small points of reality. The girl. The morning fire. His fear is raw and bottomless. He is unendingly vigilant to its movements and has never lived without it.

The girl's preoccupations are continually in her eyes. It is like watching the shadows of tiny fish flickering in water. Her constant worry for the boy. What she has seen since the city burned. The faintly buzzing sky, the random metallic sounds ringing like a tocsin as if marking the beginning of some dreadful period of torment and labour in realms of which this is only a shadow, an appearance, and beyond which a greater malice grinds methodically toward them to reveal the ineluctable terror in all things.

What is eating away at the girl's thought: that she has not experienced the worst; that outside of what she has known there is yet something else waiting, a blur in the mind, something that will come to dominate her life so completely that even to think of escape will be a punishment.

Dog and the children settle into their shape of walking, as steady as machines; a triangle with Dog at the tip, the boy trailing behind her to one side, mirrored by the girl behind him. He is contained within their watching, as Dog indexes the landscape and the girl screens him with her attention. The boy, with his stiff goose-legged gait, his head down, occasionally humming tunelessly to himself as he rocks along. The girl half a head shorter, puttering along behind him, eyes flicking glances from side to side.

The moon is a dead shell, the ruin of a world in another universe where everything is spoiled. The light flares like a candle flame in a tunnel. The children are filthy with the soot and ash that has blown on them as they slept. Dog's feet slur through the ash caked in drifts on the road. They crest the jagged edge of a hill as they leave the fringes of the destroyed city and look across a flayed landscape down a long narrow valley blasted by fire and studded with the charcoaled stumps of trees, like broken teeth bared in the jaw of a burned corpse. The sky whitens and glows and they descend into the valley. The road is a long scabrous wound.

The boy plods along behind his skeletal shadow and the sound of his boots makes a regular punch in the air. They walk among the destroyed tree stumps and the ash sucks up the light like water soaking into sand.

Dog's scant awareness is scattered across the carbonised wasteland, as they trudge under a sky the colour of a dirty bandage, a daylight moon drifting like a cinder. The boy keyed precisely into his fear, chained to it like a whipped animal, the girl resonating with the multiplication of despair, a fixed impoverished algebra stuttering on the certainty that she will burn first and that he will see it.

Far away, a pulsing column of smoke. At night, distant high-pitched shrieks like the tear of metal on metal. At dawn, a dull concussion passes beneath them, terrifying the boy and setting him muttering and whimpering, his face white as an egg. The torn ash-strewn sky is bleached of all colour, now scabbed with clouds. Throughout the day the boy looks constantly at the sky as though in fear of the clouds crawling across it. The girl stays at his heel matching her pace to his, talking softly.

They walk through grey mechanic shadow.

The road forks, one arm choked with incinerated wreckage of some kind, a repeated inarticulate signature of burned timbers and fused metal clotted with shapes like bodies, the armature of iron and charcoal crushed together. The boy mutters and flinches. The girl takes his hand and leads him down the cracked twisting road under a sky that bleeds light on them in a shroud.

The road creeps through hills like slag heaps under light that hangs like a dead flower in the sky. There are things resembling corpses scattered along its length as though dragged there and butchered, the fire coming later in its cyclonic force burning the dead and their colonies of worms, the crows in the sky bursting into flame.

The road dips, swerves through a culvert into which rain has dumped slurries of ash and sticks like carbonised bones and rises steeply through a cutting blackslabbed with rock on either side like the jambs of ancient doors bedded into the scorched earth. Here are the outer limits of the firestorm, the ragged edge where a concatenation of wind and rain threw it back on itself, dying in its own devouring, but not before it had funnelled up the road in a last incandescent shear, the trees exploding in ringed shockwaves, flaying the violent orange air with burning shards and sending vast showers of embers flaring into the night.

The fire had then vanished, evaporating into the empty sky and now Dog and the children are on the cusp of its territory as the track falters and effaces itself into grass.

The grass is long and ribbed and luminous and burns with an intense radiance like a sea of candles. Across the bright canopy of the trees there comes a dull echoing roar as the rain sweeps across the valley in a burst of live water and blooming shadow.

—

Dog and the children shelter beneath a vast spreading tree until the storm passes. Rags of mist drift like sails, their tattered edges catching momentarily on the canopy of the forest. The wind rushes through the boughs and the ragged banks of cloud lit from within curve across the world.

The children's fire flaps like a rag in the wind. The boy crouches over its little pulse of heat, smirking to himself as though at a joke he has suddenly remembered. The girl looks at him sideways through a curtain of wet matted hair filthy with ash and dirt. The sparks of the fire rush upward, sputtering through the crown of the tree. The branches seem to pull down the sky and hold the moon above them like a broken mirror that catches the light of the fire, broadcasting it across the cold land behind them. The night is pulled over their heads by the trees in their atemporal movement. Stars glow like campfires in the labyrinthine shadows above, burning and dying like torches, each ball of light rolling on its own path across a grooved sky.

In the morning the harsh diamond warbling of a bird is shocking in its impact on Dog's ears, her hearing dulled by so many days of silence. Light filters slowly around her as though rising from the very grass. Across the torched and silent landscape they have left behind, thin lines of cloud and smoke lie like old scars.

The boy lies staring up into the foliage of the tree as though transfixed, his face taut and dreamy in the puddle of his black hair. The smoke drifting across from the fire makes him look as though he is fading from sight. Sunlight ignites the songs of birds, birds they never see so that, as the days pass, Dog begins to wonder what the source of their calls is. Dog can hear a trace of running water, as if from behind a curtain. She follows that faint, definite fall to a rock face under a screen of grass down which water trickles into a damp rift choked with leaves.

Water, yes water; how could I have forgotten it? It is like remembering I am held up by a frame of bones.

When Dog returns from the spring the boy is looking into the fire that the girl is stoking and eating something she has given him. He calls a greeting to Dog, gets to his feet, crosses and, bending over her, his pale face a few inches from hers, a plate and an acorn, looks into her eyes with great earnestness and speaks. His words tumble like stones and the girl feeding the popping fire looks up startled, her eyes round with astonishment. His question floats and waits. He remains bent over Dog, nodding like an old man. Still nodding he returns to his fireside crouch. The girl looks from Dog to the boy and back again all in a long moment and then whatever is present passes.

The girl re-sorts the contents of her bag, which seems to contain a variety of indistinct objects, soft and hard. The sorting is her way of mapping the day to come and those that follow, of pacing the tempo of her mind, reordering their safety, throwing markers out into the dense atmosphere of the future, where she will find them amid the tides of sorrow and amnesia that constitute her days.

As they move into the forest it is like stepping into the hub of a great spoked wheel. In the stitchings of light that pattern the long shadows, the boy looks as though he is appearing and disappearing as he moves. Behind him, the girl, bright liquid eyes sharp with attention, thought guarding thought, hair tangled, clothes coloured by rain and ash and dust, is like something the forest has deftly fashioned out of leaves and air and humus of the forest floor to give a voice and presence to itself.

In his inhabiting of time the boy has been perfectly in step with the repetitive dull brutality of their journey from the ruined city, the pattern of days that overlapped each other as tedious and numbing as a pile of skulls, each the product of identical and mechanical execution. Cocooned in his memory is a paralysed moment secretly revisited. If every step is a repetition of the last, where will be the rupture that frees him to taste something other than fear? Where will come the word in the sentence that is not like all other words? He is aware only of the rupture in himself, the broken thing that is now in the world and that he can taste in every moment.

The children's steady insistent pace begins to slow. They follow tracks that are little more than intimations of space between trees and camp at night under a sky that is a vault of leaves and bare starlight.

They climb in slow angles down the mountain. The boy casts around them bent-backed. The girl shouts to him, commenting on his finds: the tick of water dripping from leaves; a bird call; a red fungus in a wrinkle of white bark; clots of luminous moss on wet black slate, a tiny jeweled rhomboid of light; a single leaf suspended dancing in an invisible flutter of wind; puddles of black water. It is as though he is watching himself through the eyes of everything else, perhaps even the grasshopper's compound eye, giving himself the capacity to leave himself and to return, having found within himself an unimaginable secret.

A sound like the rush of wings travels through the clear transparent gloom under the canopy. The trees rise into light.

The forest canopy obscures the day's dissolution into violent sunsets, the brimming over of which floods the sky ahead of them with portents and auguries, bloody clouds, the flash of sheet-lightning. The night rushes up out of the soil and Dog and the children are sitting around a small fire that crackles with sparks. The boy is feeding it with twigs and shreds of bark.

The children sleep and the fire glows molten and covers their sleeping forms with shadows. Dog sits under the hieroglyphic constellations, patiently gathering the disintegrating memories of the dead. It is like reading truncated stories that have been shorn of beginnings and endings and contexts.

The wind begins to rise in the afternoon, a silver shuffling in the trees that brings down showers of leaves upon them. When they reach the top of the ridge, and the forest's edge, a shallow valley is revealed below them patched with yellow areas of grass, crossed by a geometric line. The valley lies lengthwise like a thrown blanket, twisting around a wall of green cliffs, fissured with dark vertical streaks like rust. At the end of the cliff wall, a series of three great shattered pillars, as though the cliff was struck with a series of axe blows, split like a block of wood, its sections still upright held by a web of splinters.

The sky is rapidly changing colour, becoming burnished and hard as though an enormous metal plate were lowering itself toward them, blank and shining and automatic. When the darkness unfolds around them, the storm that the metal sky perhaps foreshadows has still not come and Dog and the children camp under trees that rustle uncertainly in their upper tiers without rest.

In the morning everything is still and opened up into a great silence. The bronze sky seems to vibrate very slightly as though a sound or shadow has carried across its face.

They walk out of the forest, crash through high dead grass and brown mulch, releasing clouds of feathery dust along their spiky track of noise and the road is suddenly upon them, thick with purple flowering weeds. It runs in a straight line under the face of the cliffs now standing above them, scored by an aeon of wind and rain. The light flares above them in its metal sky as though a vast caged furnace is burning.

They follow the road in its track of grass. The face of the cliffs begins to glow with light as the rest of the landscape starts its fall into darkness. And as the road fades under a sky now almost glittering, Dog sees the huge slumped outline of the machine in its field of grass and purple flower, and hears the first distant cracks of thunder. The machine's many corroded arms and pistons are fused with rust to an enormous hull that leans slightly toward them. A great metal door, buckled down its length, is jammed open digging into the earth. The machine's corroded surfaces are deeply gashed, as though they have been clawed. One end of the hull is torn open and has spilled out long entrails of rust through which the weeds now flower.

The sky is flashing with purple light and the thunder cracks in multiple stuttering explosions. In the last few moments before Dog and the children take shelter inside the machine and the storm arrives in a cataclysm of sound and wind and shattered darkness, the grass looks to be lit from beneath by an infernal interior light and the very air seems opalescent as though at the point of combustion. Darkness falls like a cell door closing. They huddle inside the ruined machine and listen as the seams of the world begin to part.

A sound as of a great hammer striking metal rings out over the top of the storm, as if, at long deliberate intervals, blows of inconceivable force are being struck at the foundations of the sky. The thunder cracks with a noise like the breaking of timber, and lightning flashes in long horizontal snaking lines like the strokes of a whip. A screech like the rending of metal from metal goes on and on without pattern. The darkness is absolute. Dog waits for the sound of rain, the rain that gives any storm a sense of time, of shape, of the passing of events. But there is no rain. There is just the layered screaming of the air and the sky and the light, shattering above their heads.

The machine shudders continually. Something breaks off the outside of the hull with a deep rending sound that is instantly swallowed in the howling of the wind.

They live in a pitch darkness illuminated and fractured by the brutal tearing light that slashes at them through the open doorway and the jagged wounds in the machine's hull. The afterimage of the doorway, stamped over and over by the savage horizontal lightning, stays repeated in Dog's blinded vision. It seems to her that she is contained in some reified instant of time surrounded by doors at every point of looking, each revealing identical fragmentary landscapes of destruction, inhabitable only by beings of spectral cruelty. The children huddle together in the flashing light, the boy with his hands pressed over his ears rocking his head from side to side. He may be crying or moaning or mewling like a baby but the noise of the storm drowns him.

Time vanishes. Day and night disappear. This may be all there is and will be, the ending of the world unravelling in a prolonged paroxysm of unshaped brutality, where the structures of existence break down in titanic shuddering scales, invoked by storms of such elemental violence that all Dog has ever thought or believed, perceived or represented will be sucked up and instantly burned to a dense mote of ash, drifting in a vacuum. These are the moments in her journeys that most terrify her; that she will be unable to maintain her presence, that forces outside of her control, some linkage of causality of which she is unaware will shatter the illusion of linear progress and self-coherence and she will be blown out of the minds of the dreaming dead as they disintegrate.

There is nowhere to go of course, no final destination. But there is the possibility of change that is not like other changes, where perhaps you find yourself again but with more ability to interrupt the crushing appearance of reality, to provide some refuge for those who find themselves without one.

In the flashing intermittent light, the girl is revealed with lolling head, eyes half-turned up in her face. The boy winds his arms around her as though to prevent her escaping or transforming, or abandoning him like a ghost.

And then the storm ends. The searing light and the tensile rending noise diminish as though at the turning of a dial. It is still completely dark, a darkness that now reverberates with a relentless pressure. And when every atom of the world is housed by silence, a silence of terror and defeat, it becomes clear to Dog, clearer than a dream, that something in the structure of the world and its subtle and manifest reality is irretrievably broken, unshackled from the world's impermanence.

When light comes, uncertainly, leaking away almost as quickly as it arises, the children are asleep, slumped together, dreamless and exhausted.

The storm's cyclonic movement has stripped the sky of cloud. The grass lies flattened as though pressed against the earth, each strand displaying its pale underside. Other than the turmoil of grass there is no visible mark of the storm's passing. Perhaps because of this everything seems more dreamlike, as if at the back of Dog's mind a signal is being given that something basic in her awareness of the world has changed. It is as though the grass and the trees and the sky were of no consequence in themselves but the manifestation of something else that the storm was collapsing. The cliffs stand clean and still and sharp against a pale sky.

In the wavering light the machine's interior is a trash of broken metal and drifts of grass and leaves. The boy slowly wakes, dazed and haggard. As he unhooks his stiff arms from beneath the girl's shoulders, she tips gently forward and rolls slowly to the floor, her face pressing into the leaves and dirt.

The boy remains absolutely still. He makes no sound and his eyes are fixed on the girl with a dark pitiful terror. Her arms splay as though broken. There is a tiny dribble of spit at the corner of her mouth, her lips slightly parted. Behind one ear is a tiny pulse, a worm's slow peristaltic movement.

Her bones are like twigs. She seems almost weightless as Dog rolls her over. Her filthy pants, her cracked boots that seem so big on her thin legs, her torn jumper, the ragged layers of shirt, all collude to frame her vulnerability and Dog can see how tenuous her continued existence has been and what it has cost her to stay with them, incarnate.

The boy kneels by her side and with one thin scratched hand he strokes the girl's cold forehead over and over. He sits by her through the day and talks softly and endlessly. Dog waits.

The shadows drift in. The boy's head is in his hands. Dog shivers and notices that the girl's eyes are open. She is watching the boy in a strange measured fashion, and she watches for a long time. Then she closes her eyes.

It is the slight exhalation of her breath that jolts the boy's head upright. As he looks at her, dumbfounded, the girl's hand moves slightly, scratches her cheek and falls back to her chest. Later, as the boy sits in the doorway, staring into the sky, the girl crawls over to him and rests her head on his shoulder. When he fidgets she leans over and kisses him on the side of the mouth.

They stand in dim wintry light looking back toward the silent forest. Behind the treeline is what might be the smoke of burning fires, and beyond that the shadow of gathering rain clouds. Something sparks and flutters into the sky, peaks and arcs. There is an intense burst of light.

They cut across the field behind the machine. An eroded path of red soil winds steeply up behind the cliff face, through outcroppings of orange rock striped with the shadows of trees. The path is a jagged line through clumps of dry spiked grass and thin snaky trees with leaves that look like the eyes of the blind. A curling breath of cold air brushes past them and the grass stirs without a sound.

The children walk bent like the aged, and stop frequently to rest. The girl is silent, her eyes shadowed. They camp on a shelf of rock and before the fire is lit the girl is asleep, huddled on a tussock of grass, her body a tiny blot in the gloom.

The night drains away slowly and the rain rushes across the slope. There is no wind and the rain falls vertically, a beating deluge that saturates them and turns the track into a running red gutter. There is nowhere to shelter. They walk and walk. The rain is like a dream of falling water in which they cannot see, hear or think, an automatic rain that repeats itself infinitely across space. There is no longer any sky.

They flounder through the mud and streaming rain, the children stumbling wearily, slipping and falling in their misery like flightless birds. The track twists interminably. It is always the same path; the jagged humps of grass, the trees that crowd them like scavengers. They walk and walk and nothing changes.

The children are two thin scribbles in the gloom of falling water and light that slips away around them. In the contour of the rain's surface Dog sees a faint interruption. A vague ghost of shadow, a little tumbledown structure of timber and iron drumming in the rain, its crooked doorway choked with rubbish. The children watch silently as the rubbish turns to bones and Dog shovels through a carrion-heap of shattered limbs and mouldering cloth, flinging body parts out into the heaving rain, and they shelter through the long dismal night while the rain throbs around them.

—

Light flutters through the interminable pouring of the rain. The children are a single humped shape in a corner of the shelter. Through the broken angle of the open doorway Dog can see the scattered desolate bones, bits of skull stuck with a few strands of hair and marked with the tracings of leaves and insects. The wavering light steadies for a second and reveals a terracotta pot split by the thorny remains of a flowering plant. In a few moments Dog has made her way through the dark and ruined garden to a house standing vast and lightless and hunchbacked beneath the repetitively flogging rain. Behind it a towering shadow like a thunderhead, a tree of great age rising into the rain.

The doors of the house slump like bodies on hooks. The verandah is a litter of tables and chairs corroded by years of weather. Furniture hulks in shadowed rooms. There are drifts of leaves in the long dark passageways. Mildew patterns the walls. In a room of massive furniture and high plaster ceilings, a blackened fireplace gapes like a smashed mouth. The walls are hung with dark dreamlike paintings in heavy frames. In the fireplace, using whatever trick of the mind the girl has invented, Dog builds a furnace of broken chairs.

Pulled out of the cold ache of sleep the children stumble, groggy and shivering, through the sheets of rain.

The fire blazes and the room glows and pulses. The boy kneels in front of the bright flames. The fire spits and cracks at him, and his small frame, like a twist of wire, shudders a few times. Behind him the girl lies on the mildewed couch like a stone at the bottom of a well.

The house opens room upon room, like a nest of boxes. Every door reveals another corridor of shadow. A kitchen, a cold flagstoned floor, scattered with broken plates where things have run along shelves. Heavily timbered walls lined with grim cupboards. Knives lie on the surface of a table. When Dog stands on a chair at a sink marked with long brown stains, the tap grinds stiffly. The house groans and the tap coughs water the colour of dried blood.

The cupboards are filled with jars, pots and bottles, packed dim and glowing under their patina of dust. It is like some intrusion from another world, all the ways that food can be gathered and stored, hidden away and sealed as if for their coming.

The children are asleep in front of the fire, end to end on the couch, as though resting in the bottom of a rowboat. The shadows in the room flare before the fire's intent. They give a deep illumination to the enormous paintings fixed to the walls. In one, a sun in a night-blue sky breaks like the yolk of an egg and spills its yellow light onto the figure of a young girl, her face turned toward Dog, solemn-eyed as she approaches a tree that blazes in the sunlight, each leaf a raised hand gifting a benediction. In the other painting a woman sleeps under a translucent sky. The grass she reclines on is a swathe of tiny knitted shadows of great depth so that she appears to float. Her face is serene. The hill behind her rises as though about to open like a flower and reveal some mystery visible to her eye alone.

The fire eats broken furniture. In the depths of the children's dreams the objects of the house wake to their own surfaces. The battered armchairs become silent and genial inhabitants of a tiny arboreal planet gravid with its own awareness. The knives in the kitchen twitch fractionally. All the objects and surfaces that the house contains begin to take on a species of knowledge. Leaving jars of food on the floor by the couch, Dog walks through the house. Through the dusty windows the light is like milk, the treeline a deckled edge marking where the world ends.

When the children wake, Dog is sitting in a hallway by a many-windowed wall looking out into the silver repetition of the rain. The girl emerges from a shadowed door like a visitation. She looks like someone risen from the grave. Her hair is stiff with dried mud and fragments of leaves, her thin, white face masked with dirt. In her hands she holds a cup of water. In the rain-smashed glass, Dog has the illusion that she can, just for a moment, see the double-silhouette of their reflection, two joined shadows gifted with eyes. Then there is just the girl who looks at her with luminous grey eyes and slowly smiles. For one alarming moment Dog thinks the girl is going to scratch her under the chin. As the girl drinks they hear the boy's shocked and delighted laughter.

The wrecked house plunges joyfully into the rain and they might be flying, a castle in the sky, a keep on its coracle of earth and trees, shedding a stream of dead leaves in the surge of cloud and water, as the children sit sleepily by the popping, wise-cracking fire, the pulse that insinuates itself into the house's invisible armature.

For days the children sleep and sleep and wake only to eat, beginning a restoration, a concord of mind and body, grafting onto them the things which give orientation in the world; the landscapes of warmth, sleep, food and dreaming. Wherever the children go they take food with them, pockets bulging. The boy is fascinated by the play of light through the windows, the soft rain-shadowed light that accentuates everything and illuminates nothing. The girl begins to trawl through each room, returning to the fireplace with armfuls of clothes and blankets. The rain continues without pause, and it seems to Dog as though the house has freed itself from its moorings of earth and murder and decay and is flying adrift across invisible lands carrying them outside of time, behind time's workings, like a rounded dream that holds its own values of meaning and coherence.

While the children sleep in front of the muttering fire, Dog reconstructs the dreams of the house, connecting each element to another: the water-jug to the hand that made the bed; the doorway to the passing of time; the paintings to the evening's reverie on the verandah; the kitchen knives to the rhythms of the day and all these momentary objects cast from memory — the reverie or the bed or the doorway or the jug or time — all of them imagine and construct a night's deep silence, the shouts of children, the death of a lover, footsteps on the stairs, the pairing of heartbeats, the circulation of air. The house shudders.

The dreaming of the knife, the dreaming of the lamp by the bed, everything needs to be put back together in some way, at least for a little while. The long night harbours its shadows. The rain surrounds the house like a wall, hangs from its roofs like a veil. In the crowded corners of every room cower the ghosts of unvoiced memory, wretched and blind. Time stains the house with its monstrous sadness, time's colour that of the dead leaf, skeletal in its structure, blown to the back of the darkest room.

The girl finds a blackened hook fixed inside the fireplace chimney, fills the kitchen's iron kettle with water, hangs it above the fire and lays out a neat pattern of pans and pots on the hearth. She strips the boy of his clothes, balls them up, tosses them into the fire, and begins to scrub him with a wet rag. He looks like some pale wizened frog that has emerged from a lightless subterranean cave, scarified with mud and ash. As the girl scrubs and rinses, the boy mutters and whimpers to himself, but this is nothing to the panic-stricken scream he gives out when the girl makes him kneel over a bucket and tips water over his head. When she is done she throws him a blanket with an impatient word and ushers him, still wailing, to the couch where all the clothes she has pillaged from the bedrooms lie heaped.

The girl has not only revealed his frailty — his bruises, his starved ribcage and spider-like limbs — cutting away the dirt and blood and ash, but punctuated and discarded an envelope of thought, some way the boy had of looking at them. The water slops in the pots and pans under a thick scum rucked like the sloughed skin of a snake.

As white as a worm the boy wriggles under the heaped clothing, releasing a sour smell of mould and damp and earth.

The girl sits in front of the fire, chin on her knees and waits again for the kettle. Silence rises out of the air like a bubble. The rain has stopped. If the boy has not been able to act outside his broken workings, the girl has known and carried this.

She has learned to eat dust and ash. In the burned city the person that she was burned too, just for an instant, but that was enough. Exactly enough. When something burns to ashes, it burns exactly through, exactly enough. She became unrecognisable to herself and now she has to confront herself all over again, and perhaps does not know whether she can bear it, what the shock will be like.

Standing on the verandah, its floor timbered like the deck of a ship, the only sounds Dog can hear are the ticks of dripping water from the leaves and the broken gutters. They are swathed in mist. The house floats in its ring of trees. The long grass is gashed with the dark paths of running water, and reveals the shapes of fantastical objects: a small stone plinth on which sits a glass sphere, its grey eye absorbing every image from every point of view; a bench under the trees carved in the shape of a bounding cat grinning like a clown; a small lopsided figure like a gremlin, beaming sunnily from a corner. The branches of the trees drag at the ragged cloud.

The boy is standing balanced high on the arm of the couch, dressed baggily in black. His wet hair is long and tangled and he looks like some kind of eldritch fortune teller who will tell you to your face that your life is a disaster and you are going to die.

The girl's hair is tied back with a long green ribbon, hanging all crinkum-crankum down her back, and she has fitted herself with a yellow shirt and brown pants. In her eyes there is a fierce burning grief and her thin face, dusted with scratches, juts sharply out of her shirt. She will no longer have patience with suffering.

The burning fire seems to bubble through the bones of the house as if it were connected to every part of it and could articulate it all, even the paintings on the wall, if they could only discover its secret mechanisms.

The girl seems determined to do this. She walks around the exterior of the house, puzzling over something, as if the inside and the outside of the house don't fit together. She works her way through every corner and cranny of every room discovering cupboards, stairways and hidden boxes, and has a knack of making things work: bowls of glass that she cleans and reveals to be lamps; a clockwork mechanism set in the hallway walls that opens high windows; a shed filled with stacked firewood and shelves of rusting tools; the wood stove in the kitchen that when lit produces an unearthly groaning in the roof as though some slow beast were awakening, which becomes the placid but astonishing presence of hot water; a hallway that opens to a room, which is inhabited by a cupboard, which encloses a drawer that contains a box, in which are hidden a dozen small items each clouded with strange and invisible meanings, each meaning the doorway to a corridor of memory and association that tacks across time like the meanderings of a forest path.

A house can appear to dream, in its way, as landscapes do, as the forests did during their passing, but in truth the function of a house is to be a shelter for the dreamer.

The light draws the boy outside and he disappears into the garden, vanishing among the long shadows. He spends his evenings staring into the fire as if bewitched.

The girl accumulates all the items of liveliness and recovery, the clothes and blankets, the knives and kitchen tools, the boxes of ancient jewellery, and stacks them near the fireplace. In her mind she is cataloguing the interior of the house, building a structure to take them across the ocean of days that lies ahead. And from a drawer in a small bedroom, a box of coloured pencils. During the daylight hours she makes numerous little drawings on the walls beneath the paintings. They are like tiny windows, all the pieces of memory still alive within her, placed in rows like fragments of disconnected dreams. A drawing of a hairclip. A window in a bedroom. Two panels side by side, one entirely red, the other black. A woman's face. A strange shadowy drawing that keeps reversing itself as Dog looks at it: either a drawing of Dog emerging from a shadow, or the silhouette of the skull of a beast, its maw devouring a pleading figure.

The girl in the painting, under a liquid sun, looks down on the girl drawing. The girl drawing looks up from time to time. The drawings are an explanation, a private communication, a way of becoming unburdened.

Toward evening, as the sky turns grey, the boy comes in from the garden. His clothes are wet to knee and elbow. As he enters the house he gives Dog a sidelong glance, a quick slice with the blade of his gaze.

Darkness cloaks the house. Each night, with great intent, the children reinvent the practice of cooking as though they are embarking on a perilous adventure, discovering the mysterious natures of vegetables, the uncertain limits of rice, the infinite qualities of soup. And in the process the house becomes less haunted by itself, in the way that old memories of love and happiness, though painful to reacquire, can also make the images of loss we have been stuck with more bearable. The boy solemnly and seriously stirs the contents of pots, as if in a dream state, as though he will do it forever, imagining that he is the food going round and round, softening up to become something good to go inside a small boy.

The boy sits by the fire and pulls a quarter of fruit from a jar. As he bites into it his face takes on such a transformed and ecstatic expression that the girl bursts into laughter, a creaking laugh stiff with disuse. Dog grins at them both, an unfortunate occurrence that causes the boy to choke on his fruit, his eyes bulging and the girl to splutter again into laughter.

When the children sleep on the couch Dog squats on its high back and her dreams shake the house. They plunge into the sad-shadowed rooms and dissolve themselves into the air, taking residence in their oxygen. They fuse with the faded memories of the house, knitting things together in strange and unlooked-for ways. And during the long night, with a tattered moon drifting across the sky like a rag of paper, every room in the house begins to become alive with its own spectre of awareness, patched together from whatever has been abandoned, what has corroded and what has accidentally been preserved. In the kitchen it is the dialogue of knives. In the bedrooms it is the whispering of doomed hope. In the long corridors there is a brooding contemplation on light and time.

The night passes. The black windows are like mirrors. The garden crowds outside. The house fills with subterranean dreams and the firelight sends its shadows into the girl's drawings. The girl turns restlessly. The boy lies like a sunken stone. At dawn, the light is an orange smear. Shadows open up the paths in the long grass where the boy has trod and pushed his way into the garden's silent interiors, making tunnels that end in cul-de-sacs of weeds and at one point what looks like a grave, a pile of stones amid the yellow grass.

These are their days, each a season of grey and lilac cloud. Green shadow comes sleeping, dreaming into the house. From beneath the open windows comes the hooting of invisible little birds. Frogs witter and honk mournfully, glum for rain.

The girl slowly fills the walls with her draw-ings and the boy continues to disappear into the garden. In the evenings when the boy returns to the house, the girl questions him absently and he only nods his head.

When Dog eventually follows the boy he proves to be surprisingly slippery, as though he has taken the longest and most randomised route he can think of. He has worked his way down a steep slope through a labyrinth of grass and crowded woody weeds alive with insects and dust. Dog can

hear his voice before she sees him, rising and falling in its excitable lilt, the sudden fractured pauses
as though his sentences break before he can finish
using them.

The canopy of an enormous domed tree cuts
the light so sharply that the weeds and grasses
stop at its perimeter, as though pressed against an
invisible wall. Inside the shadow sits the boy.

Among the lichened roots of the old tree
he has laid the bits of skulls with their assorted
bones. They lie as though resting, the fragmented
limbs sketching out the traces of a body. The boy
talks and his hands circle and clench themselves
and sometimes he rocks silently as if convulsed
with grief, but his face is shadowed. He sits
motionless for a long time looking at his hands.
When he begins to speak again his voice is ques-
tioning and ashamed.

When Dog creeps back up the hill through the
long tunnels of grass, the boy's voice follows her
for a little while like the mournful chatter of the
birds they never see.

—

It is Dog, tracking a smell of rain, mould and
lichen, who finally assembles the jigsaw of the
house and finds the ruined library behind its hidden

door. When the door opens, it is as though she has discovered a secret garden or abandoned aquarium.

An immense branch, knuckled and scarred with age, has snapped off the tree that towers over the house and speared through the roof collapsing the shelves of books, all billowing inward in a wreckage of timber and roof tiles, torrents of books and clumps of sodden foliage. The timber of the collapsed shelving, the branch of the tree and the remains of the roof have provided a patch-worked lattice of shelter from the sun and rain so that, while some volumes have fused to each other and others have become as brittle as the shells of snails, there are many books beneath the heaps stacked like middens that have retained some structural integrity, like cages bent and twisted by intolerable pressures that still function as shelters in which things can live and breathe.

The dead leaves mingle with the heaps of books, soaked by the rain, sunburned season after season, pages sheared from their spines. Through the smashed ceiling, broken fragments of sky are revealed. The books lie like flocks of dead gulls, their backs broken as though from having been dumped in a pit. The print on their covers is like some indecipherable charm, unsettling and signless.

Dog's gaze is running over the avalanche of

books when she is pierced by something that she can't immediately register, like seeing in a crowd the face of someone you thought was dead. The terrible shock of the familiar made strange is sometimes briefly visible on the cusp of disaster, bright, luminous and clear.

She picks up a ruined book that falls apart like the body of a decomposing animal. A few random pages are still legible. Numberless days of rain have rotted its spine and much of the print has been obliterated. A few pages here and there have been partly protected by random circumstance, sheltered by broken branches or by other books, but still corroded and discoloured like dead flower heads in the forgotten corner of a garden.

Dog is terrified by the bare fact that she can read them. The syllables move themselves into meaning, but become descriptions of matters she doesn't understand, of things unimagined, that make no sense: a description of the use of some kind of weapon; a list of deteriorating weather conditions; a hideous old woman dislocates her jaw laughing while someone dies; a child falls out of a tree that then begins to burn; a cryptic theory of sanity is posited.

It is like finding a grave beneath autumn leaves after a cataclysmic storm, a storm that has blown through a hundred autumns simultaneously across time. And then under this broken sky, holding the rotting remains of the mouldering book, comes the moment that always comes, eventually, in one way or another, the moment that makes this existence possible. Dog has the sudden concrete perception that she is inside her own mind, that she has always been inside it. It is not that this phenomenal event that is 'Dog' is stuck inside another object like a rat in a trap, but that every iota of physicality, of memory and perception — the plants growing up the walls of the room, the weeds rooted in the leaves of the books, the smell of mould, the sounds that twitch across her ears, the pieces of sky — is all of a kind, all of the same taste, as though she is looking at a reflection in still water and when it ripples something of her ripples too. There is no way in which her own perception and what is perceived can be separated.

In that instant, as everything seems to be about to glue itself together, she vanishes. Dog disappears from herself. She looks for herself and her self isn't there. It is as if, looking into the world, the world looks into her, mirrors mirroring. Dog cannot grasp what she is seeing without being swallowed up, her mind flooded with its own nature.

Afterward, she remembered the moment when she first encountered the two children, her awareness tacked to a point in space — observing herself emerging, like the aspect of a dream that suddenly unfolds a hidden corner and throws one's being into a shock of sinister recognition. One sees not a stranger, but oneself stranged.

And while the memories of the house are coded in the thousands of items large and small with which it is filled, they take on a particular structure in the contents of the library, where a conscious and deliberate effort was once made to gain a binocular vision of the past and a panoramic sense of the present. The library was the place where the house was given its instructions for dreaming.

Salvaging what remains of the ruined books is like foraging among the shells of dead dreams, as though, overtaken by a catastrophe, they fled in panic leaving behind only empty husks, perfect in every way, but unanimated, like the skin of a cicada from which anything sentient has long since fled.

But it is not the recovery of a function of the house that drives Dog to excavate the library and remove those books that could still be read, but the shock induced in her by the discovery of the fragments of recognisable text. Buried among the rubble of books, Dog wants there to be annotations of her life, compendious and splendid, in text so familiar that in her mind it seems to be illuminated, bringing with it more meaning than it can contain in its syllables.

But in her quartering of the library and the methodical retrieving of books and their unfathomable contents, Dog finds no other text whose script is recognisable to her. She spends her days in the library, and it is like finding out that her own past has been stolen from her and then returned as so much trash. She is forced to return over and over to the fragments she first discovered as if they are messages sent to her by a stranger who knows her intimately, but whose intentions she cannot discern.

Yet even though the remaining images and descriptions are as disconnected from each other as different species of insects, and cannot be stitched into a linear and meaningful narrative, what they evoke in her is almost intolerable, like being thrown into a dark room and forced to listen to the voice of someone you love crying out for you and unable to find you, just as you are unable to tell them you can hear them.

The girl works at her drawings day after day and continues to reconstitute the secret workings of the house. The boy spends his days outside. And if the girl is discovering how to articulate the house, he is finding in the vast overgrown garden all the ways in which the house broke down and was gutted of life. When the boy comes in at the end of the day, he and the girl talk very little. Sometimes he has an insect to show her cupped in his hands or held in a glass. When they hear a bird call the boy lifts his finger as if to anoint something, stopping their wandering thoughts and placing them on its cry.

The nights — when they are most aware of the outside world and can often see the distant glow of fires, and hear sounds like explosions inside a bell sunk underwater — become increasingly quiet and still. At one point a high-pitched note rises in the west, faking in its first seconds the call of a bird they sometimes hear at night, before dying in a metal pyrotechnic howl and fading into the sky. And though the night sky still sometimes flickers after sunset with transparent sheets of spectral light miles high, the glow of fires behind the horizon has faded.

The remains of Dog's dreams of the dead are finally breaking up like wrecks, leaving behind a trail to which she sometimes finds herself clinging during the watches of the night, the children sleeping on the huge couch before the flickering fire, while Dog sits on the back like a gargoyle letting dreams come and go on the tide, disintegrating a little even as they pass through her. Of the dead, all that is left is the random imprint of memory. They pass through her and she knows they will never return and that she is no longer their anchor.

It seems to Dog that the world has been emptied of something, a quality that she cannot quite taste, but that is leaking away like ink from a bottle.

Dog trawls through the piles of decaying books, stacking them in the hallway like bodies. Those from which only fragments can still be saved she piles up separately like bits of broken bone. Because everything is written in languages she does not understand, it is impossible to sort them by any likeness. She may be placing books on the history of garden ornaments next to descriptions of mass murder. Some of the books Dog recovers contain pictures or diagrams, and these at least can be sorted in some way, so that books that seem to concern themselves with insects or plants can at least have company, even if, as far as she knows, one might be concerned with their extermination and the other with their survival.

The girl sometimes watches her between her expeditions throughout the house. But she seems a little wary of the books, as though they are strangers or nervous animals that might strike out without warning and need to be contained in some way, their unpredictable nature anaesthetised.

When the girl walks past the books stacked in their winding rows, she makes a slight detour, keeping a zone of safety between herself and them.

Since they have been in the house, the girl has begun to address Dog directly from time to time, as though she were speaking out loud to an imaginary friend. Dog merely listens as if she completely understood and needed to make no acknowledgment. And in fact, she soon realises that the girl has invented a name for her, a recurring sound that comes weighted with many things: longing, accusation, hope. In her uncertainty and hidden anxiety is the uneasy space where she attempts to speak to Dog without demonstrating that she is doing so, and Dog tries to understand without acknowledging. That is, the girl wants Dog to understand her, but not too much.

And though, in her reading and re-reading of the ruined journal Dog is continually troubled by the idea that she has forgotten something terribly important about herself or her origins or those she once loved, this is just a kind of false image, like a mirage. In reality, the idea that she had forgotten things of great significance is merely her memory awakening to its own damaged nature, and the knowledge that the most important things that happen to us can become so thoroughly absorbed within us that even memory cannot access them.

Amid a cluster of books on the anatomies of invertebrates, Dog discovers a volume that appears to be an illustrated bestiary, though whether the beasts portrayed are imaginary or not, she cannot tell. Dog gives the bestiary to the girl, who is delighted by it and spends the afternoons poring over it, examining its pages at great length — the horned beasts, things plumed and spangled like birds, the reptiles and serpents like the inhabitants of a zoo of the mind — tracing over the elaborate drawings with her finger. And each day when she has finished her investigations of the interiors of the house, she copies onto the walls some of the bestiary's creatures in fastidious detail, greatly enlarged. And during the night, during the children's dreaming and Dog's occasional observations of the fading worlds of the dead, the flickering shadows on the walls give a welcome liveliness to the beasts she has drawn, as though they are engaged in a wild rumpus or carnival of awakening.

As for the boy, the more absent he is during the day, camped out among the graves and the overgrown gardens, the denser is his presence in the evenings. He seems to enter the house surrounded by clouds of muttering insects, but this is just an effect of his transition from outside to inside, mud on his clothes, adhesive seeds crowded onto his sleeves. His eyes are bright as fever and slowly dim as the evening progresses and he sits silent before the fire, his thoughts scattering through the house like bees. But he loves to examine the girl's drawings on the walls, nodding his head like a sage.

Dog is certain that the tree is not the boy's only place of refuge, and that his refuges ring the house, and for each he has a different practice or activity or language or invocation. Perhaps in one are the bones, in another little cages of twigs and leaves. In another he sleeps. It is as if each were a portal between one realm and another; between the living and the dead, between terror and hope, between the past and the future, shame and love, dreams and language.

The nights begin to get colder and while the days shorten, both dawn and dusk seem to get longer, as though light itself is travelling more slowly, or the transitions between light and dark are getting wider, so that soon Dog and the children will permanently inhabit an in-between space where neither dusk nor dawn ever really end but become mirrors of one another.

Dog has thoroughly excavated the library now, the recovered books lined up in the hallways in rows as if ready for use — for dissection or construction. In the library remain only those books that are no longer books, scattered around the fallen branch as if they had dropped from it like fruit and were now returning to the earth into which they will deposit their seeds, the kernels of memory, seeds that would never of course sprout but that will at least mark the place where memories have lived and died and been imagined. The hole punched into the floor by the impact of the falling branch is a grave into which the books that are no longer books seem to be slowly disappearing, as though drawn by gravity into a world where memory undergoes transformations of which we know nothing.

—

When the boy disappears it is not until dusk that they notice. The girl stands on the verandah calling and later takes a lamp out into the garden, her light wandering through the ink of the shadows like a firefly. She returns to the house and sits by the fire throughout the night, occasionally dozing, and when she looks at Dog all her old terrors are rising up again like shadows in water.

At first light the girl wades through the grass calling softly, hopefully. A few crickets call back and forth from the deep shade. Dog finds the boy's path and follows it down to the domed tree, the girl slithering down the hill behind her. The skulls lie peacefully between the roots.

It is the hanging broken twig across the clearing that points to the boy's escape. In the weed and brush on the other side he has made a narrow tunnel, a cleft of shadow. They follow the broken twigs and brushwood, a shattered line skittering down the hillside, until they emerge in brilliant light on a slender broken road. Immediately before them at road's end is a high metal gate, corroded and broken.

Beyond the gate is an immense sea of grass, shivered by a silent wind and studded with ruins of brick and metal. Inside the gate is a grey slab of weathered stone, from which a few stumps of timber protrude like bones. Wire dangles from metal poles. Scattered among them like the carcasses of animals dead in the grass are the shapes of damaged machines, scarified with the white and charcoal marks of intense heat. The girl looks over at Dog and speaks the name she has given her. Behind them the house waits, and will wait for their return, patiently, forever. Dog climbs through the broken gate. She waits for the air to open up and crush them between slices of reality. But the wind flows slowly over them, carrying the smell of grass. The air is clear and unanimated. The grass has taken over everything, rushing like water over the stubs of the broken buildings, the litter of metal, washing over the roads and open spaces. A few saplings sprout from stubbles of brick and stone, crushing them with a slow relentless pressure that will never cease.

Dog and the girl push chest-deep through the grass that closes behind them. The earth among the roots of the grass is thick with debris. Tangles of wire catch at their limbs as if to pull them down into the soil, into the subterranean shattering of the world and its contents. Stumbling over hidden disasters, picking their way around clusters of wreckage like steel traps, unable to see what is beneath their feet, they walk in meandering patterns like ants on the back of a hand, walking as though the earth were spring-loaded, every step a precipice. Dog wonders how the boy found his way through. Perhaps he has always been looking for traps.

They climb onto a stump of brick, a platform laced with prongs of rusted metal and look across the sea of grass rippling white and grey in the unfelt breeze. A ripple of light slides across a glassy sky, the grass darkening in its depths. The girl points to another outcrop of stone and metal and she and Dog plunge back into the rivers of grass. It is like they are moving upstream in time, as if they are upstream from themselves, not moving into memory but out of memory, or parallel to memory.

The light swells in the sky and dissolves into darkness. They sit in silence on their island of ruin and listen. The wind rustles below them. The girl sits and listens, staring out into darkness watching a red moon emerge from the earth. She is a hole in the night getting bigger and bigger.

That night, for the first time, Dog doesn't dream at all. It is as though she sits under a clear moonless sky, neither listening nor watching. In the morning, the light is as warm as oil on her limbs. The faint whistle of the wind serves to outline the silence that lies across the land. It is a silence of waiting, as though the thing that has passed here, unknowable and unremembered, may at any moment return.

They move from ruin to ruin. The girl detours to every burned and rusted machine. Some have been completely incinerated, scored shells in which the grass does not even invade. Others seem untouched, their doors open, their interiors of timber and fabric sewn with fungus, their jointed legs seized and folded like grasshoppers and barnacled with rust.

The wind dies and for the first time the grass accepts the trace of their presence. The night again passes, dreamless and clear. The girl wakes before dawn and pulls Dog from her floating state. Across the abyss of darkness there is a faint yellow glow, a tiny pulse like a distant galaxy that you can only see with the corner of your eye. The sky slowly becomes pink and bloody, the grass sheaves of hacked and slaughtered shadow that crowd around them whispering.

The clumps of timber and stone and metal they pass loom over them like deadfalls, or scaffolds on which could be hung and drawn only the shapes of ill-imagined beasts, bloody and infernal, homicidal in their nature and essence. As the day fades into a white dream a mutilated shape appears on their horizon, that shows itself to be a narrow two-storey building behind a hideous tree, warted and horned. The silent building is chalked with shreds of peeling paint and carries a roof of shattered tiles.

The sky is vanishing. It is almost without colour now. On the threshold of the doorway, standing on a gouged and bitten step, the girl calls softly. She disappears inside, prepared to find anything, prepared to find nothing. All that has sustained her, cruelled so long with loneliness, is the fact that she could remember his face.

The girl's shoes scrape on the floor. The walls are streaked with dark stains. A brick stair leads up to another doorway. The girl calls again.

The boy is standing before a wall broken open to the world, a window punched through the brick. A lamp from the house sits on the floor beside him. He has his back to them, looking out into the sky. The boy turns to them. His face is calm and smooth. He beckons urgently and points up into sky. The girl questions him. He shakes his head and points again. The girl walks to him and takes his hand. The boy looks at Dog as though she is a long way off, drowning. He calls to her and points up into the sky. The girl has one hand to her mouth, but Dog cannot tell if it is a gesture of wonder or relief.

Outside the window, a wind rises and flickers, as if it were riffling the pages of a book. Then comes a noise like the roaring of a sea descending upon them.

III

Acker aches in every muscle, soaked by the rain that drenched the body left on the hillside like a coat propped up with a stick. The last images of the children flicker before her inner eye. Acker thinks back on the things the children endured together, and what she was able to bear for them, drawing it into herself like ink into a pen, a suffering that, leaving not even shadows in her mind, now vanishes utterly without trace.

She hoists her pack and swings back down the slope, crashing through the green tunnel she made with her machete. The late afternoon shadows fall down the hill and the Rocks seem to grow a little larger, already looking toward the night when everything will be revealed.

Acker sits in the cabin of the F100, lights a cigarette and watches the twilight appear grain by grain. Dusk is the door through which she passes, and if she misses it, as she sometimes does, she is trapped as if on the other side of a sheet of black glass and has to wait for the morning to find her way back.

Dusk is the liminal point. Dusk is the empty bell. What remains of the world floats like a residue of dust on the surface of water.

Acker turns on the engine and begins the long drive, the journey to the village of a few minutes that seems to be stretched out into an endless time of waiting. Acker flicks on the spotlights. At dusk they have little effect. Still, she can have the illusion that she is creating something of a haven for herself, the cabin of the truck and the smear of pale dissolving light before her. The long twilight falls like a cloud. The pure light of the day, now disintegrating, reveals its threadbare nature as though it were a thin sheet of paper slowly dissolved by black water.

It is at this time, driving below the Rocks, beneath the very gaze of the Nmbngee, through a dusk that seems endless, always falling, that Acker begins to see things. The verges of the dirt road are long ruins of shadow and the headlights of the car throw grass and lantana into flat planes of light like paper cutouts, the lantana like coils of wire around columns of ink, as if the night were being harboured or generated there, soon to pour into the sky.

A huge kite-shaped shadow flits across the road at the very limit of the spotlights. Something like a rag floats out of the void beyond and drifts past the windscreen. Things skitter and flap at the edges of the road. Acker thinks of a bestiary, *The Imaginary Creatures of Dusk*, a dusk that pours out of the rainforest in a flood. She winds down the window and over the grumbling of the engine can hear the harsh and unfamiliar calls, as if cicadas had gained the voices of crows, or owls the coughing growl of lions.

The blue night rises up into the sky as if filling a glass. The air is saturated with noise, like the voices that fill the foyer of a theatre before the performance of some fantastic and dangerous opera, where spirits inhabit the bodies of birds and people return from the dead to sing one final aria, both a paean and accusation to the living, before being dragged by invisible forces into a *bardo* of shadows and silence.

Acker drives on, slowly, steadily, as though she were driving through a crowded marketplace, like the marketplace of that very morning, and could hear the musicians, the blues singers, the bands of accordions and trombones. She rolls a cigarette with her hands draped over the wheel, the Ford trundling along in second gear. The cabin seems to be surrounded by wings, and she feels a weight in the back, on the edge of the tray, as if a gang of children were hitching a ride.

She is suddenly driving into the village, past the brilliantly lit hospital on her right, the silent darkened police station on her left. The truck swings into the carpark and as the night brims like water she closes the door of the little office, lights the candles and jabs the remote at the CD player that picks up where she left it, at Glass's 'Mad Rush'.

The Beautiful Girl's grevillea sits in the corner by the door, its single flower glowing faintly in the candlelight. Acker props her booted feet on the table, draws on a cigarette and thinks through the day. And in the place where her thoughts would usually pile up like wreckage Acker tacks them neatly to each other, end on end. She rehearses the conversation she will have with the young woman in the morning. It is the matter-of-fact truthfulness that is always valued. Yes, I walked with them. The girl still had her habit of scratching her head impatiently when puzzled; the boy still sometimes chuckled to himself as though he were playing pranks on everyone in his mind. I watched them sleep.

But it is only as Acker begins to cut and shuffle the tarot cards that she realises with a certain cold shock that the woman was not just grieving for the children but also for her.

—

The village drifts suspended, lit up like a bathysphere, surrounded by constellations of winged and floating skeletal shapes, a carnival of regret, where to lament means merely to know who you are, what you have done and how the world appears. As the light disappears, sucked away into the Rocks, gathered into the deep skirts of Blue Knob, the village's empty footpaths become mysteriously covered with dark grass. In the shadows of the buildings, in the seamed and jointed and many-angled jumble that is the street front, dark transparent figures move, constructing the ordered preparations. The twilight falls like a thin curtain suspended between the village and the Rocks, and the vast fissured cloud of Blue Knob sealing the village and diverting the straight linear ruler of time. Lights flicker into life on both sides of the street, suspended in the air. The darkness beyond turns blue.

It is not the dead arriving but the ghosts of our living selves.

The village shopfronts, so chaotic by day, are now transformed, emptied and filled with shadows, their dimensions shifted in some way so that they become more diffuse and difficult to contain within the gaze. Out of the moonless sky come the lights of concocted flying things. And if we had not just eyes but eyes stolen from our dream lives, perhaps we could see them drifting slowly over the streets, loaded with their cargoes of the unbodied, all cleaving to this boundaried space where time has somehow hollowed itself out and become porous in order for this collection of rickety structures for the living to reveal itself as the place where all the ghosts of our living selves try to regain the objects of memory.

They disembark as though on a welcoming shore and their voices are like the sound of animals running across the naked strings of a piano, and the street becomes crowded with familiar figures that at the same time are distinguished by their alien silhouettes. Beneath the night's great lens of silence the first meetings take place on the street, a traffic of unknown tongues conjuring images that flicker like light passing through the spinning blades of a fan, meetings that will continue deep into the most inaccessible areas of the night before dissolving at dawn with the first breath of cold air drawn in from the Rocks.

The thousands of lamps that float above the street chitter to each other like wrens. And if we were able to observe them closely, we might see within them worms of the kind that burrow beneath the skin of a corpse, glowing with a faint lunar radiance, absorbed in arguments grave and recondite passed on over thousands of generations, confirming the nature of a world that is always richly decaying, attended to and watched over by the beetles and worms and other microscopic creatures that devour it and within it lay their eggs.

Their talk, of course, is not something to be revealed here, or at least not yet. It is often mordant and ironic, and if we were able to eavesdrop we might discover the conversations that we could have with each other — you and I, you and those you love — that could help us to divine what we previously thought impossible to know: the ruined nature of each other's hearts.

The conversation of corpse worms is like a dialogue in a two-handed play. They nod to each other, solemn as old priests, mouths thoughtfully chewing. They make a lot of jokes too, but they are dry and private and therefore not suitable for exhumation.

The illuminated street of the village floats like a window in the night, so bright that perhaps even the Nmbngee looks out to see how the whitefellahs are coping with death, with shame, their compulsion for stealing his people's children, and their strange and complex ignorance.

Things are just beginning. Yes, they are just beginning as the lights go on. It is as if the surface of a lake were suddenly lit from beneath, revealing myriad swarms of previously invisible and unimagined things, so numerous and uncounted that if the lights blinked out for a few seconds, one would be left with after-images of inexhaustible repetition, a profusion of beasts and wonders and floating radiozoa, iteration on iteration clouding the mind with uncontrollable dreams.

The seamless sky, now scattered with limitless stars that only an absent moon can reveal, fills with silent winged vessels.

As the shades and ghosts of the unremembered past sail toward the village, the stages for the performances of the bitter miracle plays, brilliantly set and formally presented, appear under the glowing lamps, a circuit of plays that will revolve through the village deep into the night. The one with all the jokes about the angels. The one about the ghosts. The one about the gargoyle. The one about the sky filled with black sunflowers.

The angels, all shoddy wings and brimming eyes, lurk in nooks and crannies — the abandoned cars rusting beneath the lantana, the old cow bails

— beetling out into the world to attend to children's scraped knees, to stop the bottoms falling out of shopping bags, or to watch with helpless tears the head-on car crash, the rolling semi burning. And needless to say when confronted with massacre or the daily murder of children and their mothers or the vicious politician's persecution of the wretched, they are bloody useless.

The ghosts, stiff and pale, strange as robots, emerge like flies where the sky cracks and collapses, and they spread across the land driving bunyips before them in clouds that eat everything, even the children.

The gargoyle, crafty and sardonic, performs stand-up to an audience of priests, badly disguised as minor demons from hell. When it gives them mock absolution at the end of its routine, all the priests explode in geysers of slime and are revealed to be petty demons of hell in the form of priests, disguised as petty demons from hell.

And in an imaginary sky the black sunflowers, massed like stormclouds, draw toward them, with an inexorable gravity, through light like water, all the stolen children into the embrace of the Nmbngee, while their persecutors shrivel like burned insects.

But these will only be the preliminary acts that play as the shops and the streets fill with voices, and the cast-off shadows of the living arrive by every contrivance. Much later, after one of the Aunties has strode forward to give the Welcome to Country, will come the main performance, *sans* angels or devils, and the sidewalks and the skies will be filled, the lights dimmed, and even the corpse worms will become silent and attentive as the children enter and begin to tell the story about the lost writer and her sorrow and anger.

But first, between the carnivalesque crowding of street and sky and the later theatre, there are still many sorrows to be laid to rest. Just because you're dead doesn't mean everything is finished. Everything is lost, it is true, and nearly every activity we engage in comes to naught except sorrow and anguish. But still, all of these have to be spoken to, because it matters how you die.

—

The night spins like a top. Acker knows that the night, as always, will be long and she will navigate it, as always, like a coracle in a storm. As always, she seeks her window into the night, to see in through the glass of the bathysphere. She lays out her cards. Roadkill, crossed by the Buddha of Compassion.

Holy fuck. There's no way I'm going out tonight.

And in the tiny office walled with books, she will tonight at last finish constructing her *Ars Moriendi*, her protocols on dying, the project she has been working on for so long.

She glues in the final image and inscribes the title page. 'The art and craft to knowe ye well to die.' It is not a *bardo thodol*, a book that speaks to the dead about being dead, but a book that speaks to the living about being dead, as if the only way to understand what it means to be dead is to remember where you are. In the end it seems to Acker that she has constructed a book of jokes. As if it were ridiculous to act as though one weren't already in a *bardo*.

Acker flips the book over vertically to write its verso title, which she does deftly in the faux gothic script she has perfected: *Amor Mundi*. She smiles to herself. Almost laughs out loud. It's a perfect figure eight she thinks. You enter a doorway and find yourself emerging from its mirror.

I live in a world of ghosts, she thinks, and I've been the only solidly existing thing.

—

We dream and shape dreams and are made by dreams. There is nothing in this world that is not a result or function of our dreaming. Each of us is a point of dreaming, the source from which dreams proliferate and take shape. We dream profoundly. There is no other way in which we can dream. On the mind's surface dreams swirl like oil, our days unfolding as a dream's efflorescence.

At sunset each day, the Rocks blaze for a few seconds with a roseate light that is almost too bright to look at, even as the Rocks themselves cast long dense shadows across the valley. The light lies horizontally across the sky. The balance of light and shadow suspended, the massive silhouette of the Rocks, the bowl of the valley with its odd distinct twist, skews the perspective so that it seems to Acker that she is simultaneously gazing down on the landscape from a great height and across its width. The dusk comes down infinitely slowly and gently. The Rocks stand out sharply for a few moments against a sky the colour of crystal.

Okay, let's begin again.